mama's trippin'

Katy Watson-Kell was born in Scotland and moved to Western Australia when she was ten. Her ancestry is a melting pot of Australian, New Zealander, Irish and Scots — she is a descendant of an Irish convict girl transported to Sydney in 1828 for petty theft.

After leaving high school on a whim, Katy talked her way into a smorgasbord of occupations including golf course attendant, handbag seller and professional luncher until her creative juices finally bubbled to the surface. She lives in a lakeside Fremantle suburb with her husband, four children and Hiro the cat.

*To Pat,
Bon Voyage...*

mama's trippin'

Katy Watson-Kell

KATY WATSON-KELL

Hope you enjoy!

Fremantle Arts Centre Press

Australia's finest small publisher

First published 2006 by
FREMANTLE ARTS CENTRE PRESS
25 Quarry Street, Fremantle
(PO Box 158, North Fremantle 6159)
Western Australia.
www.fremantlepress.com.au

Copyright © Katy Watson-Kell, 2006.

This book is copyright. Apart from any fair dealing for the purpose of private study, research, criticism or review, as permitted under the Copyright Act, no part may be reproduced by any process without written permission. Enquiries should be made to the publisher.

Cover Designer Adrienne Zuvela.
Typeset by Fremantle Arts Centre Press
and printed by Griffin Press.

National Library of Australia
Cataloguing-in-publication data

Watson-Kell, Katy.
   Mama's trippin'.

ISBN 1 921064 07 2.

I. Title.

A823.4

Publication of this title was assisted by the Commonwealth Government through the Australia Council, its arts funding and advisory body.

For Dave and Angelina

*In honour of karapuna —
the Moriori ancestors*

She's got this great dirty laugh, my mum. Just bursts right out in the worst possible places. And sometimes, when the joke is extra filthy, her eyes expand; her mop of dark blond hair flies back, then this obscene cackle erupts from deep inside her. Which is why, I suppose, after everything that's happened, there's an ache in my heart — I know I've got to find her ...

For the tenth time in half an hour Von studies the face of his mother. She looks about sixteen in her cut-off jeans and boob tube, but she'd just turned twenty-four when his father took the photo. Like his few faded memories, her features are slightly blurry. They were at their secret place out the back of Mundaring, sizzling sausages for breakfast. His dad still drives him there, mostly in winter. They huddle around their makeshift BBQ, and sometimes when he stares into the mist around the pine trees, her face almost comes back to him. Almost, but not completely. The photo was taken the week before she left. That was over ten years ago — he imagines she'll look older now.

She promised to meet him at Wellington Airport. Said not to worry, she'd be there waiting. But the plane's been down for more than an hour and he's feeling like a dick as he hovers by the Coke machine. Now his eyes start clouding over. Faces blur into a wave of muddy confusion. Being diabetic is a pain in the arse — stress can sometimes trigger a hypo. He sucks on a barley sugar, lets the glucose do its job. The clouds begin to clear and a pale moon emerges; two dark craters are staring straight at him. She's slim — no, skinny — and she's gawking so much that he wants to run away. Then a flash of lips and teeth rip the moon in half and now she's all over him.

'Von?' she asks, like she's not quite sure of herself. Then she laughs out loud, grabs his hand fiercely. 'It has to be you; I'd know those eyes anywhere …'

'Mum?'

'Mama, you used to call me, when you were little. Mum's okay, or Charlene, if that's easier.' She laughs again as she squeezes his hand. But behind the bluster, he can feel his mother trembling. Maybe he should hug her? Isn't that what sons are supposed to do when they meet their long-lost mothers? But he's frightened to hug this tiny, bird-like woman — scared that she'll break in his big, clumsy arms. He'll stand there holding her and the weight of all those missed years will close in and crush her. The air will slip out of her. Then she'll be gone forever.

Excusing herself to Von, Charlene rushes into the toilets. She slumps over the sink and splashes her face with water. When she reaches for a towel, the dispenser is empty. A quick rummage in her bag — not even a tissue. Glancing in the mirror at her dripping reflection, she sees the unlined face of a girl. Could she really have given birth to that towering young man? He's still outside in the foyer waiting for his mother. But she'd imagined him as a kid, a skinny teenage kid — over the last few days she'd been studying her old photos. As it turns out she could have saved herself the bother — she'd have known those eyes anywhere. Rich walnut brown but in a softer light they seem almost green. They're the only thing that hasn't changed a bit. He's not as solid as his dad but he's got the same golden skin. She's relieved he didn't inherit her freckles. He was only six when she left, it's not something she feels proud about. Her choices had run dry and she couldn't take him with her.

She rubs her hands together and crouches beneath the dryer, letting the warm air evaporate the moisture from her skin. After touching up her lip gloss she takes a deep breath. Her nerves are still jumping but it's time to face her son again.

They're in the taxi heading for Charlene's place in Cuba Street. It's already past midnight and he's dying for something to eat. Charlene hasn't said a word since she hopped up front with the driver.

'Where's Stella?' he asks about his little half-sister. Seconds tick past before he gets an answer.

'Left her at a mate's place.' He's resenting this conversation with the back of his mother's head, but Charlene appears to have ESP. She swivels around with a megawatt smile that matches the flash of her tiger print jeans. 'She wanted to come.' Her pale blue eyes drill through him. 'But she gets a bit tricky if I keep her out late.'

'Can't wait to meet her!'

'The feeling's mutual. She's been hyped-up all week, driving me mad with her big brother's photo. But you'll get to catch up soon. Kristie's dropping her home first thing in the morning.'

The taxi pulls over in front of a row of shops. Charlene fumbles through her bag but she doesn't have the money. The cabbie glares sourly in his rear-view mirror.

'Sorry,' Von shrugs, 'only Aussie money, mate.'

'Wait here,' Charlene orders as she dashes down an alley. A few minutes later, after satisfying the driver, she leads the way up a rickety fire-escape. She unlocks the door, flicks on the light. 'Sorry about the mix up; must have grabbed the wrong purse.' She examines him again and he finds himself fidgeting. 'I'm surprised,' she says, quite matter of factly. 'I've always imagined this mini Jack. But now, all grown up, I don't see much of your dad in you.'

You don't look like your dad. This is ice-breaking waffle. He trails Charlene to the back of the apartment.

'Your pad!' she announces as she draws back a drape. There's a fold-up camp bed with a turquoise blue Transformer quilt, a tatty pine chest and a psychedelic lava lamp.

'You used to love Transformers!' She plumps up the quilt. 'I couldn't resist this when I found it at the discount store. But I guess you've probably outgrown them a bit.'

Charlene seems embarrassed. He tries to reassure her.

'They're still pretty cool. One of my mates has a Transformer tatt. As long as it keeps the cold off — it's bloody freezing in here.'

'Yeah, much colder than Fremantle at this time of year. I'll fire up the heater then we'll crack a couple of beers.'

Beer? That's interesting. He was expecting Coke and Tim Tams. But she's not exactly your regular mum — she was definitely weird at the airport. She'd only just said hello when she disappeared into the toilets. And what about the *rock chick* get-up? She reminds him of a Video Hits Flashback — all big hair, black lace and skin-tight denim; an alarmingly thin hybrid of Kylie and Madonna. The Transformer thing's cute though. Fancy her even remembering.

He dumps his stuff on the bed while Charlene gets the beers. Things feel strange and he needs to be careful. After unpacking his kit, he gives himself an insulin shot.

Charlene's waiting on the couch, the beer's already opened. Soon they're clinking bottles together as they feign a mateship that doesn't exist yet. 'So,' she says, brightly. 'How's things?'

'Good,' he replies. This really is excruciating. 'The flight was okay, but the wind gusts were insane when we came down in Wellington. Had a huge chuck when I got off the plane; I'm starving now though.'

'Wait right there.' She reminds him of Zebedee from the Magic Roundabout as she bounces off the lounge then lands in the kitchen. The apartment, if you can call it that, is mostly open space. And the kitchen is tiny — really just an alcove. He watches his strange new mother as she burrows through her cupboard. She eventually re-emerges with a huge bowl of corn chips. 'There's dip in the fridge — I hope that fills the gap.'

He feels self-conscious munching away in front of her. Charlene takes the odd sip from her Lion Brown — she doesn't look comfortable.

'Listen,' she says finally, after swallowing a yawn. 'Let's call it a night. We'll catch up in the morning.'

'Yeah, cool,' he agrees, a bit too brightly. They're both relieved. The first night is over.

Lying awake in bed, Charlene's not sure what to do. Should she be Von's friend or try to be his mother? She'd hoped their reunion would be exciting, special. But now, she realises, that was asking too much. Ten missing years can't be fixed in one evening. There'd been so many times she wanted Von to join her. But when she picked up the phone, she couldn't dial his number. That was before her rollercoaster years — dark insane years when Von faded from her memory. Then a new child came along. Life seemed almost normal. She was keeping her nose clean and being a good mum to Stella. But demons find a way of creeping back in even if you're sure they've been exorcised forever.

A solitary tear trickles down her cheek as she relives the moment when Von first moved inside her. She remembers grabbing Jack's hand, laying it on her belly. Soon she's dreaming of the boy she had to leave behind. She sees him curled up in bed, perfect and peaceful. But then her dream child rolls over and Charlene cries out in her sleep. Her little boy is scarred. His soft, golden skin wears angry red scald marks.

Someone's picking his nose. Strange but true, it's happening. He's lying there, not properly awake and there's a finger up his nostril. It tickles at first but soon he's in his own private version of *Alien*. A wriggly probe is heading straight for his brain. A weight sits on his chest and he finds it hard to breathe. But whether it's fear or exhaustion, Von's eyes refuse to open. Nails dig into his nose, sharp and painful. Then comes the scrinch …

'Ouch!' he yells. This is pure unadulterated agony. But the Torturer persists as she perches on his belly, her busy little fingers are checking out his molars. Forcing his eyes open, he studies his tormentor. Enormous brown orbs bore straight through him and the intensity of her gaze says he's under investigation. She levers herself off his tummy then disappears momentarily. A second later she's back, holding out a photo. She gives a shy half-smile, her eyes shining with excitement.

'Hello,' Von says to his little sister Stella.

There's a sharp, icy draft and he's grateful for his embarrassing, but warm, Transformer quilt. He smells eggs and bacon cooking. Charlene makes funny, tuneless sounds as she stomps to the music that drifts up through the floorboards. It's hard to control a sudden sting of tears. Bittersweet emotions begin to overwhelm him. He's noisily blowing his nose when Charlene waltzes in with a tray and a smile.

'Breakfast,' she announces. 'Sounds like you're catching the dreaded lurgy.' Her hand reaches out — touches his brow. 'Were you warm enough last night?'

'Yeah,' he says to please her. 'The quilt really kept the cold off. It's just a few sniffles. I'm always blocked up in the mornings.'

The fry-up breakfast looks and smells delicious. Von doesn't have the heart to say it's off limits. Everything's strictly low-fat since his diagnosis. Rabbit food's a pain, really screws his head around. Who enjoys being stuck with salad when your mates are downing pizza? At first he tried to hide it, especially from his girlfriend. Juice didn't need to know that he had some freaky illness. Secretly though, he was scared; he thought he'd probably lose her. But he was wrong. Diabetes didn't faze her.

After breakfast they flick on the telly. Stella plays with her toys while she watches the kids' shows. Charlene's quiet at first. But then she gets chatty.

'I'm rapt that you came; thought you wouldn't want to know me.' She pauses for a moment. Her eyes look troubled. 'I feel so bad about everything — what happened when you were little.'

He's disturbed by the way this conversation's heading. It's far too soon. And he can't understand why she's beating herself up. If she feels so guilty now, why did she leave him? His dad always told him she'd gone on a trip. Said she needed time out — that meant a lot to a six year old! But late at night when Von couldn't sleep, he'd scare himself sick imagining what might have happened. He was sure his mum was dead but no-one was game to tell him. The whole world was pretending just to keep him happy.

'That's history,' he says. 'I thought you'd probably carked it.' Charlene looks shocked. Now he wishes he hadn't said it. 'Only joking,' he adds, trying to laugh it off.

'I hope so,' she snaps.

It was a dumb thing to say. Now they both feel awkward. When Charlene first rang and asked him to come to Wellington, Von had felt confused; he wasn't sure he wanted to see her. But things were ratshit with Juice and his dad was going on holidays. He just wanted to escape. That's why he agreed to meet her.

Smiling at him now, she doesn't look so anxious. 'You're brave,' she says, 'travelling all the way to New Zealand. It's been such a long time — it's great you came to see me.'

'It's nothing,' he says. 'I just wanted to meet the rug rat.'

The words thud out before he can stop them. Charlene looks like she's been punched in the jaw, her face all blue and grey as it slowly crumples in on itself.

'And you,' he says, too late. It's a poorly sticking bandaid. 'You of course, and Stella.'

The Torturer abandons her colourful blocks, toddles shyly over to him. Her soft little fingers wrap around his thumb. It's the tiniest hand he's ever held. When she tries to pull him up, he turns to Charlene for guidance. She's still looking shattered but nods her approval. Stella shows Von the door that leads out to the fire-escape. The wind is bloody freezing — his polar-fleece shirt might as well be nothing. Stella's still in her pyjamas, her bare feet turning blue. He tries coaxing her back inside but she'll have none of that. She stands her ground, shakes his hand away crossly.

'Aren't you cold?' No response. With steely determination she starts dragging him down the stairs. Then she makes him sit down on the cold iron step. Von's teeth start to chatter but the Torturer seems unaffected. A tatty family of dolls is tucked between the railings — dolls with missing limbs and mad, colourful, punk rocker hairdos. Stella reaches for a Ken doll in a cute fur mini and hands him to her brother like she's offering a gift.

'Thank you,' Von says. 'Thanks very much, Stella.' As they walk back up the steps, he notices the drop. For one sickening moment he imagines Stella falling, tumbling over the rusty railing until she crashes, with a thump, onto the unforgiving concrete two floors below them. It seems a dangerous place for a little kid to play. But for Stella the fire-escape is her own enchanted garden.

A rush of icy air floods into the apartment. The kids make a beeline for the radiant heater.

'Bit chilly out there?' Charlene still feels raw but she tries to sound casual.

'And you reckon this is spring!'

She sips her black coffee and changes the subject. 'How's your dad these days?'

'He's okay, I guess — pretty hectic. He's either flat out with lectures or hitting the beach at Leighton. There's a uni break now so he's up at Gnarloo Station. He likes to get away with his sailboarding buddies.'

Hearing about Jack stirs old affections in Charlene. He's probably the only person who ever really 'got' her. Leighton Beach was their second home. Von was only two or three when he learnt how to swim there.

'It's strange,' she says to Von. 'Your dad's from here, but he's living in Freo. And somehow or other, I've ended up in New Zealand.'

'I guess,' Von answers, 'but he wouldn't move back. There's a problem with his mum, that's why he keeps clear of Wellington.'

Charlene nods. 'They fell out when you were a baby.' Jack flew home to Wellington after his father passed away. That's when the rift developed — there was conflict over the funeral.

'Earlier this year he nearly visited the Chathams. I wasn't keen so I'd arranged to stay at a mate's place. But Dad was over the moon when he finally booked his ticket. In the end he had to cancel because of some stupid crisis at uni. It was shithouse,' Von explains, 'he's always wanted to see the islands.'

'I'm surprised he's never been; it's where his people came from. And yours, of course,' she adds. 'You should make the effort to go there.' Charlene jumps up, starts searching through a dresser. She returns with a pouch and hands her son a fang-like object.

'What is it?'

'A shark's tooth; it's over forty million years old. I found it at Blind Jim's, this place on the Chathams.'

'That's amazing,' Von says. 'What were you doing on the islands?'

Charlene laughs. She's enjoying their new connection. 'Pete, my boyfriend, used to deck there on the cray boats. Whenever I got the chance I'd go across with him. I've always been curious about your Moriori ancestry. And it's beautiful on those islands; wild and very isolated.'

'Dad's mentioned a museum. He said there's Moriori stuff there.'

'That's Te Papa,' Charlene says. 'It's right on Wellington Harbour.' Jack was a natural born teacher — she loved hearing about his people. And he worked so hard to get his PhD. 'Your dad's a wizard on his history — you might follow in his footsteps?'

'If my grades don't improve I won't be studying anything. Next year I'll try harder — Year Twelve's definitely make or break time.' Von tries to hand the shark's tooth back to his mother.

'Keep it,' she says. 'It's a little piece of your homeland. Something that old has to be lucky.'

The phone starts to ring. Charlene rushes off to get it. Von studies the ancient shark's tooth, imagining where it came from. He's completely blown away. Charlene's been to the Chathams. And it's weird the way she talks about his dad. She seems to think he's cool, but if she liked him so much, why did she leave him? Maybe she did love Jack and it was Von she couldn't handle. She's still on the phone but she's not saying much. And when she speaks it's in low, muffled tones. Now she gives him a look like he's earwigging in. He leaves her in peace, retreating to his bedroom.

It's a strange set-up here. Charlene's room is self-contained and there's a tiny, box-like bathroom. But the rest of the apartment reminds him of a cavern. The lights are always on — the place has no windows. She's created some divisions with pieces of solid furniture; swathes of bright fabric hang from the ceiling. His 'room' is framed by a long kauri bookcase, the wall behind his bed and a curtain of lush green velvet. A lamp shines through the green creating a foresty glow. Von feels like a four year old in his first bush cubby. But velvet doesn't provide much of a sound barrier.

Charlene's increasingly heated barney is hard to ignore.

'He's not here!' she says for the umpteenth time. She slams down the phone as he wanders through to join her. She's on the floor now, cuddling little Stella. More to comfort herself, it would seem — the child's totally absorbed in the fights on Jerry Springer.

Charlene lets go, releasing the Torturer. 'Sorry about that, but you didn't need to hide.'

The tone of her comment annoys him. It feels like a put-down. Not sure what to say, he decides to stay silent. Charlene looks embarrassed. She's digging at her nail polish. But after a few awkward moments she's ready to chat again.

'So, tell me about your girlfriend?'

He'd love to say *mind your own business*. But she's waiting, quite sincerely, so he finds himself answering.

'Things are cool,' he says. 'But for a while there we kept fighting. It was my fault,' he adds. 'I had all these hang-ups about my illness.' It's not easy explaining his relationship with Juice — seems like he always had the hots for her. But she's in love with her sport and she's so damned ambitious. He often gets the feeling that he'll always come in second. He used to have dreams about playing professional footy. Then he copped the diabetes — he started to feel threatened. Juice kept going from strength to strength. Von's life was total chaos.

Charlene nods her understanding. 'I'm sure it must be stressful adjusting to all that.' She gives him a cheeky smile. 'Is she cute?' She's sitting cross-legged on the worn Persian rug — an excited little girl waiting for her ice-cream.

'Yeah, she's hot,' Von says, embarrassed. 'Jenna's her real

name but everyone calls her Juice. She's an athlete, a sprinter.'

The phone rings again. This time Charlene doesn't answer. Her eyes dart away, searching anxiously for Stella. She's on her feet now, fidgety as a cat. She stops in front of a hand-painted mural. It's a curious scene to find here in Wellington. A bright, child-like vision of Fremantle Harbour, complete with frolicking whales beneath the old traffic bridge. The phone stops ringing. Charlene's still lost in the mural.

'Did you paint it?' he asks, trying to regain her attention.

'Yeah,' she replies. 'I wanted to make a window. I was thinking about you — we had great times in Freo.'

He wants to reach out and hug her but a part of him is scared. Frustration and rage keeps welling up inside him. If things were so great then why did she leave him?

Charlene searches for answers in her strange painted window. No more putting off. She's going to have to tell him.

'That was the cops on the phone. They're after Peter.'

Von looks shocked. He responds with confusion. 'But I thought you said he works on the cray boats.'

'Did I?' Charlene mumbles. 'Well, he used to work the boats — I keep hoping he'll go back to it.' Von waits for more. He knows she's being evasive. 'Pete was hanging out with a bloke he'd decked with on the Chathams. He likes to party, always brings his friends home. But with this guy, Rob, it was different; Pete never let me meet him. I had a feeling in my gut they were up to something dodgy. He told me in the end — they'd set up a lab together.'

'Pete's a scientist then?'

Charlene fights her irritation. This is hard enough, without Von being a shit-stirrer. But she doesn't react, just tries to answer calmly. 'You might call him that. He was cooking methamphetamine. Pete used to do a bit of dealing. Just small-time stuff, that's how I met him. But everything changed when I fell pregnant with Stella. We made a fresh start, gave up the drugs.' She watches her son, tries to gauge his reaction. He gives nothing away as he sits on the couch in silence.

'Things have been tough since Pete took off. He's not a bad bloke, just easily led. He's a great dad to Stella — spoils her rotten. That's the trouble, he's always blowing money. I have to work nights to stay on top of the debt, but now there's no-one to look after Stella.'

Von slowly stands up then, panther-like, starts pacing the room. Charlene jumps when he turns around to face her.

'What the fuck is going on? And why did you ask me here?'

The rage in Von's face startles Charlene. She retreats to the landing and lights herself a cigarette.

Von blames himself that she's screwing with his brain. This is the woman, the so-called mother, who so easily disowned him. Now he's wondering whatever possessed him to come here. Charlene comes back inside and stubs out her cigarette.

'Hungry?' she asks, as she butters some bread for sandwiches.

'Yeah,' he replies. But it's hard to think of food when his mind's a mess of questions. Charlene still seems agitated. She attacks a tin of tuna with a rusty looking tin-opener.

'I've wanted to see you for such a long time. And I know you must wonder why I've never bothered. But I had to make things right. I was desperate to show you I could be a proper mother.'

'I'm not six any more. I don't need a lot of mothering.'

After forking out some tuna, Charlene spreads it over the bread. 'But I'd made a fresh start — I just wanted you to see that. And I thought you had a right to meet your little sister.' She hands Von a sandwich and a Coke to wash it down with. 'Things were going great when I asked you to come over. Who would have dreamt all this shit with Pete would happen.'

Von tries to ignore all the holes in what she's saying. Charlene seems sincere. He wants to buy her story.

'So what's Pete been up to?'

She sips her Coke then sits down on the carpet. 'It's a mess,' she says. 'They cooked all this crystal meth, much more than they could move. But Pete knows a lot of bikies; he started shifting drugs at bargain basement prices. Only one problem though, he forgot to tell Rob. They had so much stuff stockpiled, Pete was sure he wouldn't notice.'

'But the guy caught him out?'

Charlene nods. 'And he expects his share. Business is business.'

She explains how Pete got in a panic when he couldn't produce the money. Then he held up a service station but his face got caught on camera — he had to do a runner. Charlene's eyes look moist as she picks up little Stella. 'The cops harassed me for days; they reckoned I was involved, and then Welfare thought Stella would be better off in foster care. Now I'm worried sick that Rob is going to find me.'

'You should talk to the guy. Maybe come to some arrangement.'

Charlene gives Von a look like he's said something stupid.

'I can help,' he explains. 'Dad gave me extra cash in case I fly to the Chathams.' He still feels guilty for taking the money. Jack suggested he should go; he didn't want to hurt his feelings. His dad's passionate about their ancestry but Von doesn't feel the same. He's an Aussie, end of story. It's hard to feel connected.

Charlene shakes her head. 'I earn good wages — I'm not asking for your money. But now that Pete's gone, there's no-one to care for Stella while I'm working at Endorphin.'

The implication behind her words couldn't be clearer. After ten years of absence she says she's ready to be his mother. She's also in a heap of strife. There's no way that he can trust her.

'So let me get this straight. You invited me here because you need a babysitter?' Stella's fast asleep, draped across Charlene's shoulder.

'It's not like that!' She won't look Von in the eye.

'Oh, yes it is!' he yells, charging out of the apartment. The woman's full of crap. He can't deal with what he's hearing. As he flies down the fire-escape, he wonders where he's heading. But soon his mother's footsteps come crashing down behind him.

'Stop,' she pleads. 'I know this looks bad but I promise it isn't like that. I really want you here. I wish you could believe me.'

Von turns around to face her, certain she's lying.

'Please,' she begs. 'I only need a few weeks. Just till I get enough money together. I'll find Rob and pay him back — we'll be free of him forever.'

'But I told you before. I can help with some cash.'

'I know,' she says. 'But we're talking thousands and I need to do this my way.'

They move back inside. Charlene puts Stella to bed. It would seem her revelations are over for the moment. Crashing onto the couch, Von starts thinking about his father. If he flies home now, he'll just spoil his dad's vacation. He feels embarrassed and let down — Charlene asked him here to babysit. What a low act. It hurts too much to think about.

Charlene wipes the mirror clean, starts putting on her make-up. As she readies herself for work, it's Stella she's worrying about. Von looks twenty but he's a sixteen-year-old kid. What would he know about caring for a toddler? She's desperate though, and better Von than leaving Stella alone.

She checks her reflection from every possible angle. Dance work's hard to get when you're competing with teenagers. She remembers being that age — overblown with confidence and crazy ambition. Growing up in Sydney, she'd set her sights high. The Sydney Dance Company was her ultimate goal. Years of classes at the academy were rewarded with a scholarship. She thrived on hard work, always put in the hours. She had the perfect dancer's body and at fifteen still enjoyed the lean, boyish figure most of her friends had swapped for curves. But when Charlene's boobs finally sprouted and her periods arrived, everyone had to know she was officially a woman. To mark the momentous occasion, she threw a huge party at Bondi Beach to celebrate. She carried a surfboard under one arm and wore tampons for earrings. Her girlfriends thought she was a mad, crazy bitch and loved her all the more for it.

Around this time her dance instructors started niggling, often dropping clumsy hints about too many chockies. Charlene just laughed. She never worried about her figure. But one day during class she was asked to step outside, and was told, very bluntly, that she had to lose those kilos. She remembers running home, stripping off in front of the mirror. She'd always loved her body and the athletic way it moved for her. She had changed now and she liked her fuller figure. But the longer she stood there staring, in her mind the larger her body grew. Later that evening she took her first pill. No-one needed to know and the instructors wouldn't care. As long as she got thinner ...

Now, staring in the mirror, Charlene knows that nothing's changed. She's still obsessed with her weight, never happy with her figure. When she was pregnant with Stella she put on a few kilos — probably because she gave up amphetamines. But she can't delete those memories; she's tormented by her triggers. She still longs for that powerful, energetic feeling. *Speed = Confidence = Anything's Possible.* Might be the Baby Animals in the CD store beneath her; a song, a smell, can take her back to that time. She has to fight hard not to reach for the phone and Von's insulin kit hasn't helped either. Using all her strength, she clears the junk from her mind and turns her troubled thoughts to more pressing worries. Throwing on her coat she leaves the steamy bathroom.

'I usually get home just after two-thirty. Here's my number at work, but only call if it's an emergency.'

Von takes his mother's card as she waves bye-bye to Stella.

'You be a good girl for Vonny. Mama will be home soon.'

Vonny. Where did that come from? 'It's Von,' he tells his sister as soon as Charlene's gone. Not that he needs to worry. Stella hasn't uttered a word since he landed here.

He rifles through his bag, pulls out his PlayStation. It's been a stressful day and he's ready to zone out. A few minutes of setting up and it's all systems go. Soon he's living like a gangster in the world of Grand Theft Auto. Stella stares at him longingly. She'd love to have a go. But she's only two years old — there's no way that she could play him. He returns to the game. Stella keeps on staring. Then she climbs onto his knee and hijacks the controller. The kid is amazing, an incredibly quick learner. She's got a PlayStation gene that manipulates her fingers.

Von feels a bit unnerved; now she's mixing it with drug dealers — happily splattering pedestrians and frying people with a flamethrower. What if his sister grows up to be an assassin or a terrorist?

It's time to take a look at Stella's bedtime ritual.

- *8.30 pm. Quiet time. Read a story for about ten minutes.*
- *8.40 pm. Help Stella brush her teeth.*

- 8.50 pm. Take Stella to toilet. Put on night time nappy.
- 9.00 pm. Tuck Stella into bed. Sing a little lullaby.

If he gets her off to bed, he can play more Grand Theft Auto. It's nearly eight-thirty, time they got started. He turns off the PlayStation. Stella's bottom lip crumples. Quiet time, Charlene said. But the apartment is so silent it feels positively spooky. Rummaging through his backpack he finds his Journey CD. Trent Humphries is a muso who busks around Fremantle: his gentle dulcimer sounds are great around exam time. Trent's music starts to play. Stella brightens up again. Von searches for a book but she doesn't seem to own one — they settle for a TV mag he unearths in the toilet. She's keen at first, likes looking at the pictures. But soon she gets bored; now she's fiddling with his watch strap.

Ten minutes are up. They head for the bathroom. There's a Mickey Mouse toothbrush which he quickly spreads with toothpaste. After popping it in her mouth, Stella sucks it like a lollipop.

'Don't eat it,' he yells, prising Mickey Mouse off her. She runs away and hides in her pink tepee bedroom. Stella's makeshift room is definitely a tepee, having a more conical design than Von's simple green cubby.

'Nappy time, Stella!' He's trying to sound cheerful. Charlene showed him what to do by demonstrating on a dolly. But Stella's not a plastic toy and now he's feeling flustered. She refuses to keep still — Von's convinced he'll never manage this. He starts singing 'Humpty Dumpty', hoping to distract her. He feels like a stupid dork — thank god his mates can't see him. A few versions later, he's mastered the Velcro strips. But as soon as he turns his back, he hears them both go *rip* again. It's not hard to work out why — the Torturer's soaked her nappy. He completely forgot to put her on the toilet.

There's a full bag of nappies so he grabs a fresh one. Stella's running out of steam — this time she doesn't fight him. She just stares at Von sadly with those huge brown eyes of hers.

'Hush little baby, don't you cry, Vonny's going to sing you a lullaby …' Moments later she's snoring on his shoulder.

He tucks her into her tepee then flops down on the carpet. The PlayStation beckons but now he feels exhausted. His mind's in turmoil as he tries to make sense of things. He keeps wondering why he's here. Is he just his sister's nanny? Unfamiliar noises jangle and unnerve him. Charlene's fridge is part lawnmower and a pendulum clock ticks annoyingly in the background. He gets an overwhelming urge to rip out the battery. But using all his self-control, he turns the TV on instead. He's just settling into a show when the phone rings loudly.

'Hello,' Von says softly, trying not to wake up Stella. Nobody answers. 'Hello,' he tries again, a little louder. Someone's there. He can hear raspy breathing.

'Yeah, g'day,' a guy answers. The accent's pure Aussie. 'Is Charlene home?'

'No, she's working. Can I give her a message?'

'She's right, mate. Just let her know the Seagull has landed.'

This conversation is getting more than a little weird.

'Landed where?' Von inquires.

'Like I said already, mate' — the Aussie's sounding tetchy — 'the friggin' Seagull landed. Doesn't matter where, right, but the birdie's found his roost.'

'Okay,' Von says. 'I'll pass that on.' This has to be Pete. The Seagull thing must be some crazy code name.

'How's my baby?' Pete asks. Von assumes he means Stella. But he's not convinced he should be chatting to this guy. Charlene told him herself that Pete's running from the law. And she hasn't really said how things stand between them.

'She's okay,' he replies, 'probably sleeping at the moment.'

The Seagull's voice softens. 'She's a pearler, ain't she, mate? Any chance I could have a word with her?'

'Stella's just gone to bed. Maybe Charlene can call you later.'

'Don't mean to be nosy — but how long have you been seeing her?'

'I'm her son,' Von says, embarrassed. 'I guess Mum's probably mentioned me.'

Pete hesitates for a moment. 'No, mate, don't reckon she has. But that's Charlene, ain't it, always full of secrets.'

Pete seems all right in a blokey kind of way. When the line drops out Von feels a little sorry. There's no-one else to talk to — he was glad to have some company. Stella's only little. She'd have to miss her dad. At least Jack stuck around, but Charlene's a total mystery. It's strange to think they once had a connection. A sudden chilliness starts to overwhelm him, like the icy shock from a dive into the ocean. But when he thrashes his fears around, no warm relief comes. Just a cold, hard slap of knowledge — she so easily dismissed him. The Seagull just confirmed it. She erased Von from her life.

Charlene scrambles onto the podium, rejecting the tacky advances of a way-too-friendly punter. She always forgets when she pulls on her hipsters. Guys often go the grab if they spot a bit of G-string. Her eyes are shut as she tries to find the groove. Some nights it's easy — her body flowing with the tides of electronic music. But tonight she's feeling stiff; it's going to be a long one.

She opens her eyes and takes in the scene. Away from the dance floor people sprawl across huge pillow seats. They're mostly into speed and a smorgasbord of amphetamines. Water, not beer, is the drink of choice. Others get their high from the trance-inducing music. Charlene studies the sea of dancers. They're predatory, tight — eyeing each other off. She feels detached up here, high on the podium. Goddess-like and unattainable. Endorphin's a classy gig. The grottier clubs make you dance in your lingerie. But here they like their girls in ultra cool street chic. Sexy, but in a slow burn kind of way.

The strobes are disturbing. They frazzle Charlene's brain. She lets her eyes wander until they settle, momentarily, on a Japanese anime flickering across a suspended TV screen. The cartoon transports her straight back to childhood — to Astro Boy and her first true love, Kimba the White Lion. Losing herself now, she smiles down at a punter. The guy's obviously a user, his lips all raw and nasty. Speed's a bastard like that; it sometimes makes you chew yourself. Charlene's seen him here before, she'd lay odds that he's a dealer.

At the end of her first set, Charlene's neck tightens painfully as she remembers Von and Stella. She hopes that her son stuck to the routine. Stella's usually no trouble but she can trip out occasionally. She grabs a seat at the bar; sips some iced water. The speed freak from the dance floor has sidled up beside her. He's up again, down again — a bundle of twitches.

'Can I get you a drink?' he suddenly blurts out. Charlene hesitates for a moment. Dancers aren't encouraged to get friendly with punters. But she needs to watch her pennies, can't afford to buy herself one.

'Yeah, okay mate,' she answers. 'Why not? I'll have scotch on the rocks.'

Later, on the podium, the whisky lubricates her mood. She feels a nice, buzzy warmth pumping through her veins and can tell, by the upturned faces, that she's putting on a show. At last her shift is over. After clocking off at the bar, she enters the biting cold of Vivian Street. The night is fine, there's no need to call a cab. If she takes her usual shortcut, she'll be home in ten minutes. As she turns the corner into her alley, she hears a sound not far behind her. Someone sniffing their nose or stifling a sneeze — Charlene glances over her shoulder but there's not a soul to be seen. Relieved, but cold, she pulls on her hood. Then she flicks on her torch as she climbs up the fire-escape.

It's exactly two-thirty when the door bangs shut. The first thing Charlene does is check on sleeping Stella. Von hears gentle, nurturing sounds as she whispers to his sister. Something about those noises tweaks a string of memory. Did Charlene whisper to him when he was a baby? He senses kindness in his mum — a softness struggling to ooze out from beneath the brittle surface. She rustles about in the kitchen then, for one worrying moment, he's sure she's going to check on him. But soon the toilet flushes. Her bedroom door clicks shut. Thank god she's back home; now he'll finally get some sleep. It's been a long, lonely night babysitting the Torturer.

The alarm goes off at eight. Morning's crept up far too quickly. Through a gap in the curtain he can see his little sister. She's sitting cross-legged, glued to the television. She's probably getting hungry; doesn't look like Charlene's surfaced. Von knows it's up to him to cook the kid some breakfast. He climbs out of bed and goes to the fridge. There's just some stale looking bread, eggs and a tub of butter. Stella tugs at his jeans while he's whisking up the eggs. She obviously wants to help so he lets her have a go. Soon she's spray-painting the kettle with slippery yellow polka dots.

Charlene's door creaks open. She wanders through to join them.

'I'm ravenous,' she announces as she plonks down at the table, 'must have burnt a zillion calories at the club last night.'

'What d'you do there?' But she's oblivious to his question. When no answer comes, Von starts loading up the toaster. He thought she'd want to help but now she's staring at the television. He tries to stir the eggs while he spreads their toast with butter.

The food looks and smells delicious when he sets it on the table. Charlene must be hungry — she greedily wolfs down her breakfast.

'I needed that,' she says. 'Thanks, I really mean it.'

Von tries to fake a smile but the steam inside is rising. Last night was bad enough, now he feels like Jamie Oliver. She's sitting there smugly, not a worry in the world. Next she'll be asking him to do her dirty laundry. He takes a deep breath, tries to chill his mood a bit.

'Did you find the Seagull's message?'

'What a space cadet,' she says, 'using code names and everything. Pete's mates started the seagull thing. He even got himself a seagull tatt. I don't suppose the bastard told you where he's hiding?'

'No, just that he'd landed, whatever that means. But he asked how you and Stella were going.'

Charlene looks annoyed. 'Nice to hear he's thinking about his family.'

'He didn't know you had a son,' Von can't help adding.

She looks embarrassed, upset. He wishes he hadn't said it. She gets up from the table, heads straight for her bedroom. Her instant withdrawal throws him for a loop. He thought she'd be hanging out with the Torturer.

'So?' he enquires, before she shuts her door. 'What about Stella?'

Charlene eyes him strangely as she points at the TV. 'If you want to go out, she'll be okay. Try not to stress. Your sister loves her telly.'

She goes back to bed. Von's torn by what he's feeling. This sucks; it's not his job but he can't leave little Stella. She's only two years old. Something seriously bad could happen. But there's nothing worth watching when he channel-surfs the telly. All the kids' flicks have finished, now they're stuck with American talk crap.

'Hey,' he suggests to Stella. 'We could go and see some ducks?' He loved feeding birds when he was a rug rat. There's a bag of crusts at the back of Charlene's freezer. He scrapes off the frost and sticks them in his backpack.

Stella scurries about in her tepee and returns with a pair of sandals. After helping her buckle up, it suddenly dawns on him that she's still in her PJs.

'You'd better get your clothes on.' But the child's not impressed. She drops to the floor — throws a proper wobbly. 'Come on,' he says, 'you can't go out in your PJs.' He nearly passes out when he peels off her nappy. It's a thudder. Saturated. The smell is atrocious. He can't believe Charlene left her like this. There isn't a bath, just a trough next to the washing machine. He quickly fills it up, swishes a bit of soap around. Stella splashes about madly until the bubbles disappear. Half an hour later they're ready to go again.

Von's eyes rebel, blinking painfully in the sun; it's been far too long since he last saw daylight. Stella quickly gets distracted by her punk rocker Barbies and it's a dawdling journey to the bottom of the fire-escape. He hesitates for a moment, not sure where to go from there. Then he spots the short alley that runs through to Cuba Street. The grungy sounds of Shihad are thumping from a music shop. Maybe someone in the store knows where to find a duck pond? As he's browsing through some music, a Rasta looking guy ambles towards him.

'Hey, man,' he says. 'D'you need a bit of help?'

'Only looking, mate — I've just moved in upstairs.'

The guy ruffles his dreads, looks a bit worried. 'Not too noisy are we?'

'No way,' Von reassures him. 'The music rocks. But I'm new to Wellington — don't know my way around yet. The kid was feeling bored. Thought I'd try and find a duck pond.'

The Rasta scribbles out a map of some places where there's bird-life. 'You can check these out, but just ask if you need more info. I'm Henry,' he adds. 'Rock up anytime, eh, we're neighbours, right?'

Taking Stella by the hand, Von heads north along Cuba Street. There's a lagoon up that way, and hopefully a few ducks. They walk very slowly. The toddler's steps are tiny. She keeps staring at passers-by with those intense brown eyes of hers. He can't help wondering when she last had an outing. Soon they're wandering through the Cuba Street Mall. Irresistible smells waft out of a café.

'Are you hungry?' he asks. But Stella won't make eye contact. She's totally lost in a street juggler's performance. Colourful skittles fly above her head. She jumps up and down as she desperately tries to catch one. The busker sees an opportunity and makes her part of his show. She grins from ear to ear as he juggles all around her.

After rescuing her from the busker, Von stops to buy a doughnut. Stella takes a couple of bites before handing back the leftovers. She's had enough of walking, is starting to whine now. When he picks her up and sits her on his hip, she scrambles up his back determined to have a piggyback. His pack's already overfull, but somehow she manages to clamber onto his shoulders. They weave around the Town Hall till they reach Civic Square. A raucous street theatre is playing out its drama. Stella suddenly shouts out in a husky little voice — *Ball! Ball!* — and Von nearly falls over. They're the first words she's uttered since he came to Wellington. There's an amazing silver ball suspended in the air; a huge global sculpture of delicate metal fern fronds. An old lady stops to talk, attracted by Stella's excitement.

'Beautiful, isn't it — the Silver Fern Globe.' The lady chats away to Stella, telling her she's gorgeous. But when the old girl asks if she's Von's first, he has to stifle a laugh and explain that Stella's his sister.

'Well, she's a dear wee thing. Make sure you take care of her.'

Charlene climbs out of bed. It's already gone midday. She usually catnaps, keeping an ear out for Stella. But Von being around must have made her relax — it's the first time in weeks she's slept really deeply.

The place is so quiet, no TV or stereo, just a muffled song drifting up from the music store. She splashes her face, throws on some comfy clothes and groggily makes her way to the kitchen.

She finds the note Von left on the fridge. Stella must have been bored; they've gone out exploring. Charlene boils the kettle to make a cup of coffee. She's amused when the egg splats turn into mini-omelettes. As she tries to sponge them off, she starts thinking about Pete's message.

At least, for the moment, she knows he's safe. Why did it have to go wrong, this investment in their future? Pete was only double-dealing because he wanted to buy a house, a place near the sea — a home for little Stella. But when he disappeared their investment went with him. And it's only a matter of time before his dealer partner catches him. At least Pete was smart in one thing— he never brought the bastard home.

Rob'll need to do his homework if he's ever going to find her.

They're climbing the steps to the City-to-Sea Bridge. The Torturer's hell-bent on doing this unaided. She's about halfway to the top, making very slow progress — the stairs have brought out a stubborn streak in Stella. The bridge is awesome, with huge Maori wood carvings. His dad's mad about this stuff and Von wants to get a photo. He's just whipped out his camera when Stella turns about and starts her slow methodical march back down the steps. Now she's chewing on her tongue, a study in concentration. Forgetting about the carvings, Von takes a shot of her instead.

Soon the choppy grey lagoon spills out before them, but there's not a duck in sight, just a flock of well-fed pigeons. Stella gamely chucks her bread when the pigeons muscle in. She stirs up old memories of a day at Bibra Lake — Von was only small, wouldn't have been more than four, and he felt so brave feeding the huge black swans. Then, in a shower of hisses, one nipped him on the cheek. He just stood there in shock, howling like a baby. But Stella's made of sterner stuff. She's already reaching out for another crust of bread.

'All gone,' he says, shrugging his shoulders.

Stella looks at him in disgust. Throwing herself on the ground she starts kicking and screaming. Von's suddenly aware they're surrounded by tourists. They all stare, accusingly, in his direction. 'I didn't touch her,' he wants to yell. He tries to pick her up, but arms and legs are everywhere.

'Look!' he says, trying desperately to distract her. 'Look, Stella, *doggy!*'

She stops kicking, thank god, and he prays that there's a dog somewhere. The tourists have lost interest, temporarily satisfied that he's not a psycho child basher.

After Stella's insane antics, Von feels totally wasted. He finds a park bench, quickly bribes her with a lolly. She seems calm enough now as she twiddles with his backpack. He can't say the same for himself — he feels anything but cruisy. Then, just when he thinks babysitting couldn't suck more, the Torturer starts choking on her half-eaten lolly. He pats her on the back, tips her head forward. A sticky lump of gloop lands right on his trousers.

Her lids begin to droop; it won't be long before she's sleeping. Von's wiped out too. He decides they'll stay and rest for a while. There's a fantastic view right across the water and Te Papa, the national museum, is just a short walk away. His dad asked him to visit the Moriori exhibition there. Von's sad for his ancestors and the atrocities they suffered, but he finds it hard connecting to that past. The Moriori, the Chatham Islands, they're like a chapter lost in time. He was born and bred in Australia — his home is back in Freo. But his dad will be disappointed if he skips the exhibition. And Te Papa's an awesome building; it wouldn't hurt to take a photo.

Charlene's feeling worried, can't keep her mind on anything. She tried zoning out in front of the TV. Then she flipped through a pile of out-of-date magazines. Now she's perched on a stool, nervously gouging the polish off her fingernails. It's after four o'clock. The kids still aren't home. They've been gone all day and not a word out of them.

    Sliding back the green velvet drape, she enters her son's temporary bedroom. His insulin kit is laid out on the chest. Now her heart starts racing with unwelcome longing. Some things never change — syringes make her twitchy. As she turns away, her anxiety rises. Her mind trips out, starts playing frightening games with her. She's afraid that Rob might have snatched Von and Stella. Inhaling deeply, she tries to calm down. It's a stupid bloody thought — she knows she's being irrational. They're probably lost. Von won't know his way around; he's fresh out of Fremantle. She should have stayed up instead of sleeping half the day. He must have felt hurt — her just leaving him in limbo. Once again her eyes drift to his kit. She feels out of control and utterly useless.

She remembers, too well, mainlining methamphetamine — the incredible lift, the heightened arousal. But the temptation only lasts for a second. She has to stay straight if she's going to care for Stella. It's nearly three years since the pregnancy test showed positive. Charlene shudders at the memory — she so easily could have lost her. She'd been partying hard, knew her baby might be harmed. But after eight weeks of punishment, that tiny spark of life had somehow clung on, fighting. And Charlene kept praying to a higher power to protect her unborn baby.

When she broke the news to Pete, he was like a little kid, his face a teary collage of fear and total happiness. As he kissed her rounded belly, Charlene knew there was no choice. Soon they'd both made a pact to give up amphetamines. Her mind returns to the pain of withdrawal, to those agonising weeks when depression nearly drowned her. She could never survive that torture again. So why, she asks herself as she plays with a syringe, does the memory of that rush always light her up?

Charlene charges out the door and snatches Stella off him. She reminds him of a bull — all overdosed on aggro. Poor Stella was asleep, now she's wide awake and screaming.

'I've been scared out of my brain; gone all day and not a word out of you!'

'We went to feed the ducks.'

'Why didn't you call me?'

'No credit,' he replies, trying hard to explain. 'And I didn't have your number.'

With a tiger grip on her child, Charlene disappears into her bedroom. *Selfish* and *stupid* are muttered in Von's direction.

Dumping his bag on the floor, he's furious with his mother. She sleeps all day, just forgets she's got a kid. Then she cracks the shits when all he did was help her. They were late getting back because he checked out the museum. Thought he'd make his dad happy, fill in a bit of time there. The Torturer kept bolting, which made things pretty hard, but eventually he discovered where the Moriori things were. While Stella was playing a game unzipping the pockets on his backpack, he got a chance to look around — she was happy in a corner. The reef canoe was amazing, and all the ancient artefacts. It was incredible seeing the wing-span on the massive royal albatross. He was reading through some blurb when a Maori guide showed up, holding Stella in one hand and an insulin pen in the other. The guy didn't say a word but his eyes were shouting *'Idiot!'* Von felt like a total loser for leaving her unattended.

Charlene's out of her bedroom now. She seems a bit more human. But Stella looks upset — she's reaching out to hold him. Reluctantly, Charlene hands the Torturer over.

'I was worried,' she says. 'All this trouble with Pete, it's making me paranoid.' Her voice sounds rough. She shakily lights a cigarette.

'There was nothing to do here — I didn't mean to scare you.'

When Stella coughs, Charlene stubs out her smoke. After checking her watch, she starts fussing in the kitchen.

'I need to start dinner but there's nothing in the fridge.'

'Don't worry,' he says. 'I'll cook us something healthy.' But instead of being pleased, his mother looks offended. 'It's the diabetes,' he explains. 'Blood sugar levels. Fried food's great but it's not the best thing for me. Why don't I grab some gear from the twenty-four-hour deli — the one across the street from that nasty looking piercing shop?'

'Flesh Wound,' Charlene says. 'That's where I got my nipple done.' Von can't help blushing; did he really need to know that? She's reaching for her purse. 'Here, you'll need some money.'

'My shout,' he says, handing over Stella. Before he heads off, he scratches down a number. 'I'll get more credit for my mobile — that way you can always reach me.'

Then he steps outside and tries to stop shaking.

Striding to work in the cool evening air, Charlene checks her reflection in every passing window. Von's dinner was great, but she's not that big an eater. She's acutely aware her stomach is bloated. Deeply lost in thought, she jogs around the corner. Someone hits her with a thud — now she's sprawled across the pavement.

'Sorry, sweetheart. Didn't see you coming.'

At first she feels embarrassed but soon she's overcome with anger. This clumsy Rastafarian who just knocked her off her feet now has her cradled in his arms — he's trying to rock her like a baby.

'Put me down,' she insists. 'I'm not a bloody doll.' Feet back on terra firma, she brushes off her clothes. She was already late for work, now this idiot's made her later.

'I know you,' he says, running along beside her. 'You've been in the store and you're a dancer at Endorphin.'

'Really,' Charlene puffs. 'There must be hundreds of stores in this part of Wellington.'

'No, honest,' he says. 'It's the music store, man — I've seen you in the alley.'

When she reaches Endorphin, Charlene stops for a second. For the first time since her tumble, she gives the guy a decent gander. He's got kind green eyes and he does look familiar.

'You're that kid from downstairs — the one who always wolf-whistles!'

Henry's been sprung. He tries to feign innocence. 'Who me?' he protests. 'Never, mama, that would be bad manners.'

Charlene gives him a look, convinced that he's lying. 'I'm late for work and my boss is going to kill me. If you quit perving, you might see where you're going!'

'Here,' says Henry, as he scribbles out a voucher. 'Come into the store, pick anything you want. It's kinda my way of saying I'm sorry.'

Charlene shoves the crumpled paper into her pocket. She finger combs her hair as she enters Endorphin. 'Thanks,' she says as she turns around to Henry. Then she bounces up the stairs, her feet in perfect time to the thumps of pounding music.

After Charlene leaves for work, Von starts the nightly ritual. It's only seven-thirty but Stella's eyes are bleary. Looks like he's in luck — she might be ready for bed early. This time he remembers to sit her on the toilet but he's still a total klutz at putting on her nappy. She hasn't brushed her teeth but one night's not going to hurt her. Soon she's fast asleep, tucked up in her tepee.

At last he's got some time to write a quick note to his father. He pulls out the postcard he picked up at Te Papa.

Hey Dad,

Just thought I'd let you know I've been to Te Papa. I saw the reef canoe and this enormous stuffed albatross, and all these nifty tools they used back in the old days. You'll have to get over here — you'd like the exhibition. It's been weird with Mum though — she's having a few problems. Her boyfriend, Pete, has done a runner and I'm helping her out with Stella. Mum works at night so I'm doing all the babysitting. But my sister's okay — it's

nothing I can't handle. I've run out of room so I'll phone or email later.
Love ya,
Von

He sticks a stamp on the postcard then crashes on the sofa. He's just nodded off when he's woken by loud knocking. At first he's freaked — doesn't know if he should answer. Charlene never told him she was expecting any visitors.

'Who's there?' he yells, getting up from the sofa.

'Henry,' comes the reply.

At first Von draws a blank, but then he remembers. It's the Rasta guy he spoke with in the music store.

'Hi neighbour,' Henry says, as the door slowly opens. 'Hope I didn't wake you.'

'No worries, mate. What can I do you for?'

'Nothing, really. But after you left with the little one this morning, I started thinking.'

Curious now, Von's not sure where this is heading.

'Well, you're new to Wellington; thought you might need a mate to show you around.'

'I'm pretty tied up with Stella.'

'Your girlfriend's kid?'

'Hell, no! Stella's my half-sister, Mum's kid.'

'No way,' Henry laughs. 'That hot-looking lady couldn't be your mama?'

Von's hackles start to rise. This guy looks twenty, tops. What's he doing checking out his mother?

Henry picks up the vibe; immediately back-tracks. 'Sorry

man, no offence intended. Don't get me wrong, I wouldn't crack on to her.'

'Wouldn't want to,' Von snaps with mock severity. 'Glad we got that sorted.'

'Listen, I won't hold you up any longer but I've got a spare ticket to a rock event on Sunday — some great bands are playing. Might give you a taste for our Kiwi music.'

'Daytime Sunday?'

'Yeah, it starts at twelve; goes right through till late.'

'I'll check with my mum.'

'Cool,' Henry says. 'Come and see me tomorrow and we'll work out the details.'

Von listens to Henry's boots clunk back down the fire-escape. The guy doesn't seem too bad and it might be okay to kick back with some music.

Things couldn't have panned out better. Sunday arrives and Charlene's not working. When he hears Henry knock, Von goes to find Stella. She's playing with a school bus on the floor of her tepee. She looks at him shyly; hands him a toy wheelchair. He pushes it up the ramp, onto the school bus.

'I can't stay,' he explains. 'I'm going out with Henry. But remember, if Mama goes to bed, you're not to go outside. Stay in here and watch the telly.' This is scary — he's not sure she understands him. As he tries to stand up, Stella grabs his leg. She won't let go — doesn't want him to leave her. He calls out to Charlene but she's doing the talk with Henry. She's cracking all these jokes like she's known the guy for ever. Von finds them smoking on the landing. He might as well not be there.

'Can I have a word?' he asks his mum, politely.

'Sure,' she says, but she keeps her eyes on Henry.

'In here,' he says, a bit more forcefully. A few minutes later, she joins him on the sofa. Her expression is dark when he hands the Torturer over. He thought she'd understand. God, he's sixteen years old. It's the first time in days that he hasn't had to sit for her. He can't wait to cut loose — he's been itching to get out of there. But now, unexpectedly, he finds himself hovering.

'What?' Charlene asks, a picture of confusion.

'Nothing,' he says, finding it difficult to explain himself. But then the words blurt out. 'Are you going to keep an eye on her?'

Charlene glares at Von. Once again, she feels insulted.

'It's just that sometimes when you're asleep, Stella unlocks the door. That fire-escape's outside and something bad could happen.'

'I'm not stupid,' she snaps. 'We managed fine before you got here.' He's not so sure about that. But it's not the time to argue.

'What was that all about?' Henry's obviously puzzled.

'Just stuff,' Von explains. 'Mum likes her sleep — just wanted to make sure she'll stay awake for Stella.'

'Relax, man. She strikes me as the perfect mum.'

Yeah, right, Von thinks. Perfect for what?

A car is parked at the back of the store. It's a faded blue Camira with balding tyres — a wobbly bull-terrier nods out the back window. Henry opens his glove box and pulls out a hip flask. He gives Von a wink. 'Refreshments for later.'

He pockets his keys and they start heading for the venue.

'Had a good chat with your mum.'

'Really,' Von says, not sure how to answer.

'Yeah, she's been filling me in on a few things. She says you're diabetic; even asked me to look out for you.'

This is the kind of thing that completely stuffs him up. Diabetes is the pits but he's managing just fine — he doesn't need looking after, especially by Henry.

'Must be pretty stink, all those bloody injections. But don't worry, man. I can see you've got it sorted.'

'It's no big deal, I'm handling it.'

'Mothers,' Henry laughs. 'They spill all our little secrets. Didn't know you were Moriori, man. Had you pegged as a Maori.'

'I've got Maori blood too. But some of my ancestors were Moriori.'

Henry starts giggling. He pretends to be nervous. 'Just let me know before you get too hungry.'

'What's that supposed to mean?' Von can't help feeling paranoid.

'One of my mates, right, he's an expert on the Moriori. Reckons they were aggro little dudes that lived on a desert island. Red-headed people eaters, that's what Steve says.' Henry turns to face him, abruptly starts performing. He's doing a crazy tongue-flicking haka rip-off. Von stares in disbelief. God, he'd love to smash him.

'Sounds like your mate's a brainless dickhead.' The Moriori weren't cannibals. They banned all warfare. But he won't waste his breath explaining that to Henry. They walk for a while in silence. Every now and then, Henry has a little chuckle. Von decides to tune him out — the guy jerks him off immensely. He focuses his thoughts on the sights of Wellington. It's an incredibly cool city with an amazing backdrop of huge, green mountains. But Henry's still crapping on when they reach the Town Hall.

'Your mama's real nice.' Now he's talking in a wanky American accent. 'All the guys at work think so.'

It's time to ice Henry's wick. Von grabs him by the elbow. 'One more word about Mum and the gig's up your arse. How old are you anyway? Two, maybe three years older than me? What the hell are you doing sleazing around my mother?'

'I'm twenty-two, man. And Charlene's a grown-up.'

'But she's not a skanky ho — someone's mother you can fuck with!'

Henry shakes his head. He looks a bit disgusted. 'You're out of control, man. Think I'll bugger off, eh.'

Charlene's sitting with her daughter on the dark, cramped landing. As she rolls pink play dough into cute mini-sausages, she reflects on the chat she had earlier with Henry. For someone so young, he showed a lot of sensitivity — he was clearly sympathetic about Von's diabetes. They even shared a laugh about the way he bowled her over. If her instincts are right, he's a genuine enough guy; someone young who Von can relate to. But she's upset with her son and the arrogant way he acted. Today she discovered that Von can be pushy. Ordering her into the apartment like that, his reluctance to leave Stella. He couldn't have made it clearer — he's never going to trust her.

Stella soon gets bored. She starts clambering down the fire-escape. Charlene's heart skips a beat as she drags her off the railings. She hopes one day they'll have a safer home. Somewhere with land; a cosy beach house near the ocean. Now Stella sits at the bottom of the stairs, splashing in a puddle.

'You'll get soaked,' Charlene shouts, fully aware her child won't answer. It's usually like this; she knows she'll have to go and fetch her. 'Come on,' she says. 'You can have a nap with Mama.' A few minutes later, they're both sleeping peacefully. But when the phone wakes Charlene, she staggers through to get it.

'Hello,' she answers, trying not to yawn.

'Hi Chaz,' Bill says. It's her boss from Endorphin. 'Not disturbing your Sunday, I hope?'

You are, Charlene thinks, but she hides her annoyance. 'No worries, Bill; just kicking back with Stella.'

'I heard you were great last night. There's never any whinging when Charlene Taiaroa's on the podium.'

'Thanks,' she answers, wishing he'd get to the point.

'Listen, we're having a meeting. I have to do some reshuffling. We need all our girls here to sort out the shifts.'

'When?'

'Sorry, love, we start in fifteen minutes. It shouldn't take long, no more than an hour.'

She'd love to fob him off, but she needs to keep her job.

'Hang on,' she says, as she peeks into the bedroom. Stella usually sleeps for at least a couple of hours. She'll be back before then. There shouldn't be a problem.

'Okay,' she tells her boss. 'I'll be there in ten minutes.'

Before she heads off, Charlene unplugs the kettle. After emptying out the water, she hides it in the cupboard. She takes another look at Stella as she pulls on her coat. Then she locks the apartment door and rushes down the fire-escape.

Henry has gone. Von's stranded on the pavement. He could go home but what would he say to Charlene? *That's right; my new mate pissed me off. He's really got the hots for you!* No, that's not a good way to go, especially as she'd probably lap up the attention. He wouldn't give a fig if Henry was drooling about some chick. The guy's young, he's alive; of course he's bloody horny. Von spends half his waking life thinking about that stuff. Sometimes it's really difficult; Juice is half a world away. There's no way he'd ever cheat, but he can't go round in blinkers. Every time he turns a corner there goes another sexy chick. It's out of control — he feels like a walking erection! Henry's a cool looking guy; he could have heaps of girls his age. The whole thing makes Von sick. She's his mother — it's not natural.

    A bank of black clouds is gathering above the mountains. As Von studies the dark formation he half-notices a woman on the other side of the road. For one confusing second, he's sure he's seen his mother. As she darts down a side-street, he takes a cursory look. She's got dirty blond hair and the same fur coat his mum wears to Endorphin. But he immediately pushes the strange thought away. Charlene's with Stella back at the apartment.

In a weird sort of way he's glad to be alone. He definitely needs a break from playing happy families. It's not the Torturer's fault; she's cool for a littlie. But he didn't fly to Wellington to change nappies for a two year old. And he's sure the poor kid's silent because she needs her mum. If eyes mirror what's inside, Stella's pretty lonely. She's Von's sister, his blood; he wishes she didn't have to feel that way. Charlene's either sleeping or at work — she's not around enough to notice.

The day's turned cold and grey, perfect weather for a movie. Racing the rain, he sprints to Courtney Place. But his clothes are half-soaked by the time he reaches the cinema. Then, just as he's heading in, the hunger pangs hit. Von quickly grabs some Twisties and a Coke to wash them down with. Even diabetics need the occasional junk fix.

The Twisties have gone and the movie's total crap. But he knows, in all fairness, he hasn't been paying attention. This is one of those times when he freaks himself out. Sometimes he picks up these vibes — he feels like an antenna. His mind keeps wandering and it always leads to Stella. He's sure something's gone wrong back at the apartment.

He charges out of the cinema, running all the way home. Before he's reached the fire-escape, he can hear his sister bawling. It's not her usual cry; this is all out, terrified screaming. Von bangs on the door. Stella doesn't answer. He frantically scours his pockets for the key. But then, in one sickening moment, he remembers he didn't bring it.

'Stella,' he yells. 'You've got to let me in!'

Her screaming escalates. He'll have to kick the door in. Three boots later it finally flies open. The screams are coming from Charlene's bedroom. Stella's lying on the floor smeared with her own mess. She's been so distressed the poor kid's dirtied herself. He gently picks her up; tries to make her feel safe again.

'Stella,' he whispers. 'Vonny's here, you're okay now.'

He feels sick inside, can't stop himself from crying. This is too hard to handle, little Stella being so frightened. He's fighting off his own dark memories of being scared and all alone: the shock of scalding water; screaming for his mother. His dad eventually found him clutching Charlene's pillow. Von wouldn't let it go on the drive to the hospital. Jack kept saying she'd come home while Von breathed in the scent of her. But it wasn't enough. He just wanted her to be there.

He plays his chill-out music; waltzes Stella around the apartment. After her crying subsides, he cleans away her messes. Then he wraps her warmly in one of Charlene's jumpers. Her kisses are soft and spittley as she wraps her arms around him. She's been trapped for too long; needs fresh air inside her. She won't look Von in the eye but he knows how sad she's feeling. There's a vacuum in his heart when he thinks about Charlene. She couldn't handle him. And now she's had enough of Stella.

Once she sees the kicked-in door, Charlene flies up the fire-escape. She left her child alone; something awful must have happened.

'Stella?' she calls, trying hard to mask her fear. As she approaches the door, she hears the sound of cartoons blaring. Relief is instant — Charlene lets out a sigh. Stella's curled up on the couch staring at the television. Von shoots his mum a look. He's emanating iciness. She reaches for her child but Stella pulls away. She snuggles in to Von, starts clinging to him desperately.

'What the fuck's been going on?'

Von glares at his accuser, dumbfounded by her attitude. 'As if you didn't know. Shit, you left her all alone. You're lucky she's okay — the poor kid was hysterical.'

'No wonder,' Charlene snaps as she shoves the damaged door. 'You must have scared her witless. I can't believe you kicked the door in.'

'What d'you bloody expect? She wasn't just crying; it was full-on, shit-scared screaming!'

'But I gave you a key. You didn't have to smash it!'

Grabbing his mother's hand, Von drags her to the bathroom. A pile of soiled clothes lie mouldering in the shower.

'That's how scared she was — Stella even shit herself.'

Charlene flinches at the smell; she feels bombarded by Von's anger.

'But she usually sleeps for hours — I was only around the corner.' She halts at her own words: just like those times when she left Von. He hated being alone; he always got so frightened. Avoiding his stare, her eyes dart round the room. She's reliving that day she left the kettle boiling. She's tried to block it out but the memory still haunts her. Von was only six. She's always prayed that he'd forgotten.

'My boss asked me to come in.' She struggles to explain herself. 'He called this stupid meeting, insisted that I be there. What else could I do? If I lose this job we're stuffed, me and Stella.'

'You don't get it, do you? She thought you'd gone forever.'

Charlene takes a deep breath, has another try with Stella. 'I'm so sorry, bub — I didn't mean to scare you.' The child reaches out, ready to be held.

'It's okay,' Charlene says. 'I'm going to make things better. And whenever Mama's working, Vonny will protect you. You'll never be scared again — never, darling, ever.'

Nearly a week's gone by since the incident with Stella. And more than once he's nearly rung his father. He'd be back from Gnarloo Station — Von could fly straight home tomorrow. But whenever he looks at Stella, he hears those screams of terror. She's like a tiny shadow the way she trails him around the apartment. Won't let him out of her sight — she's too scared to be alone now. But at least he's managed to re-hinge Charlene's door. It's not a bad job; he's pretty handy with a screwdriver. It closes pretty well, but there's no way they can lock it.

Von knows he can't leave now. He feels like he's in prison. His little sister needs him but he's not her bloody mother. If he did bail out and return to his life in Freo, he'd be haunted day and night wondering what was going on with her. The years would slide by — she'd become a hazy memory. But somewhere deep inside, he'd know that he'd betrayed her. He understands, more than anyone, this is not a one-off thing. Who knows what lies ahead? Charlene might take off forever.

Her shifts are longer now; she usually finishes at three. Tonight she must be working overtime; it's already gone three-thirty. Stella's snuffling noises have kept him awake. It's hard to relax when she isn't breathing smoothly. She's been blocked up all week but Charlene doesn't seem to notice. His dad force-feeds him on kiwi fruit whenever he gets a cold. They're full of Vitamin C — great for fighting flu bugs. Tomorrow, Von decides, if the Torturer's still snotty, he'll take her for a walk and grab some from the deli.

Stella coughs and splutters then cries out hoarsely. She's not very well; her breathing sounds more laboured. Even in her sleep, her eyes are half open. She has a strange, otherworldly look that's making him feel edgy. He touches her brow; the poor kid's really burning. Little wet curls are stuck to her forehead.

He gathers her up, carries her to the trough. His dad swore by lukewarm baths to help bring down a fever.

'Don't stress,' Von reassures her, turning on the taps. 'I'll try and cool you down a bit.' After peeling off her PJs, he lowers her into the trough. She usually loves a bath, likes splashing in the water. But now she just cries and shakes uncontrollably. He pours tepid water over her curls. She seems okay with that so he keeps up the ritual. Then, just as he's lifting her out of the trough, the phone starts ringing. Stella's dripping wet, there's no way that he can answer. He quickly towels her dry and helps her into her PJs. When the phone rings again, he rushes to grab it.

'Hi,' he says. It's nearly four o'clock.

'G'day, mate, sorry to wake you.' It's the Seagull on the line. He'd know that voice anywhere.

'We were up already. Stella's not very well; she's been a bit shivery.'

'Aw,' the Seagull sighs. 'My poor little princess. You give her a hug from me — no, even better, let me talk to her.'

As soon as Stella puts her ear to the phone, her face breaks into the hugest smile ever. She doesn't say much, just a few breathy giggles. After a few seconds she starts to get wriggly.

'God,' says the Seagull as Von takes back the phone. 'This is way too hard. I can hear my baby breathing but I can't be with her.'

Stella's shivering on the couch. He'll have to cut this short. 'Listen mate, can you ring back later? Stella's just out the bath; don't want her catching pneumonia.'

'Can you get Charlene?' Pete's sounding pretty desperate. 'There's trouble brewing. Reckon I should warn her.'

'Mum's out,' Von says, alarmed. Sounds like bad news for his mother. 'But she should be home soon — you should try again later.'

'Right,' says the Seagull. 'You look after my baby. But when you see your mother, mention Kaingaroa. Don't know what to do next. Just tell her that I love her.'

Pete hangs up, disappears into infinity. What is it with this guy and his stupid bloody codenames? His accent's so strong and the phone line was bad, but Von's sure 'kangaroo' is what the Seagull told him.

Stella's temperature's still up. After rummaging through the pantry, he finds a bottle of Panadol.

'Yummy,' he says to his exhausted little sister. 'Stella drink her medicine?'

She pulls a few faces but he gets it down eventually. Now she's yanking at her ears — it looks as if they're hurting. After tucking her into bed, Von gently strokes her hair until she's sleeping peacefully. First thing in the morning she'll need to see a doctor.

It's nearly four-thirty. He hears whispers and giggling. Charlene and some guy have entered the apartment. There's a noisy clink as she grabs a couple of Lions.

'Were you hot tonight, or what?' The voice sounds rough. This guy's more than a little out of it.

Charlene chokes; she coughs up a dirty laugh. 'Just the same old routine. Whatever turns you on.'

They're way too close to Stella's tepee. As the beers clank together, their voices get much louder.

'I've got your stuff. So, how about it?'

'How about what?'

'Teasing bitch.' More laughter. 'You *know*, what we talked about.'

Von thinks back to the night after the disaster with Stella. When things had settled down, he'd given himself a shot. His insulin pen's handy when he's out and about, but most of the time he sticks to syringes. But there were only a couple left and he was certain he had more than that. For one split second he'd thought his mum was using again. Now he wonders if he was right and this guy's some kind of dealer. Von quickly sneaks a peek but they're sitting with their backs to him. They pick up their drinks and head for Charlene's bedroom.

The stranger's got a vibe that's making him feel nervous. Stella's still asleep, but she's tossing about restlessly. Soon anger erupts inside his mother's bedroom. A thump is followed by strange, disturbing noises. Part of him wants to charge straight in — grab the intruder and hurl him down the fire-escape. But instead Von takes his quilt and sets up camp outside his sister's tepee.

Lying in the total darkness, he's never felt so torn. Sick stuff's happening in that room; he wants to help his mother. But he can't leave Stella unprotected — the guy's obviously a nutter. Von's muscles tense as Charlene's door creaks open. He hears the stranger leave with a *'Thanks for nothing!'* His mother cries softly and he wonders if he should go to her. But before he gets a chance, the bedroom door clicks shut again.

She wraps herself up in a full body turban — the tightness of the blanket soothes her, makes her feel less vulnerable. Her free hand traces a trail of damaged cheekbone and she flinches in pain when she prods her swollen eyebrow.

It's been a hellish week, working the new longer shifts. Later in the night punters often turn ugly. That's when her soul caves in, she feels sucked dry and empty — just one point of crystal can help to get her through. Tonight, during a break, her friendly speed freak offered drugs, and the lure of crystal meth had proved far too tempting. The deal sounded perfect — he didn't want her money. A business one-night-stand was how he liked to view it. Her body craved crystal; she thought she'd get the deed done quickly. But after leading him through the shadows to a corner near the wheelie bins, the guy pulled away when she tried to get things started.

'It's a dump out here, kind of hard to be romantic.'

She almost bailed out; hadn't planned to make a night of it.

'It's business,' she reminded him. 'We're not getting married!' In the end she took him home. He wasn't the type to rough it in an alley.

Now she relives the shock of being grabbed by her hair.

'You're Pete's bitch,' the dealer spat. He said he knew she had his money. Charlene tried not to panic: this was Rob, Pete's ripped-off partner.

'Lighten up,' she joked. 'I thought we came back here to party.'

She can still feel the crunch of his fist against her face; see the hatred in his eyes when he forced himself on top of her. A door slammed in her mind as she shut out the pain. Then her thoughts flew far away — she wouldn't let the brute destroy her.

He didn't take long — seemed calmer when he'd finished.

'Give me a month,' she appealed. 'I just need a month, and then you'll have what my Pete owes you.'

In the rosy half-light Charlene lets out a sigh. Her favourite snap of Pete smiles out from her mirror. A sudden rush of anger starts to overwhelm her. She tears the photo down, tosses it into a corner. *Easy for you to smile! So easy to smile when you're hiding out in nowhere land.*

Unexpectedly, now, she finds herself smiling. It looks like Rob stuck to his deal. His bag of crystal meth is still sitting on her dresser.

Returning to his cubby, Von curls up in his doona. Soon he's drifting in that land between deep sleep and consciousness. It's a tranquil zone where answers often come to him. But his dreams are filled with darkness; he feels anything but calm. He's still haunted by Charlene's crying and the stranger's brutal voice, just as he was leaving.

When someone cries out, Von thinks he's heard his mother. But it's Stella waking up, calling from her tepee.

'Vonny,' she whispers when he goes through to see her. The Torturer wants a drink so he fetches her some water. He holds her tiny hand until she's fast asleep again.

Von glances at the clock — it's just gone eight-thirty. His eyes feel gritty; he needs to get more sleep. But just as he's nodding off, a foul smell fills his nostrils. He returns to Stella's tepee, finds her sleeping on her tummy. A suspicious looking lump fills out her night-time nappy. He has to block his nose. The smell pervades everything. But he can't leave the Torturer sleeping in a dung-heap. He gently turns her over, removes the offending article — Stella's eyes half-open as he swiftly wipes the mess off. Fresh in a clean nappy, she drifts back to sleep. After rolling the soiled one into a ball, he sticks it in the rubbish.

He makes himself a coffee and pours one for his mother. Then he knocks on her door but Charlene doesn't answer. Turning the knob, he takes a peek inside. She isn't there; probably off buying cigarettes. But then he suddenly sees it, sticking out from a pile of messed-up bedding. He feels six years old again as he stares at the used syringe. Now the Torturer's tiny footsteps are padding up behind him. Quickly closing Charlene's door, he carries Stella to the kitchen. She picks at some toast but she doesn't seem that hungry.

He keeps thinking about his mother, wondering what was going down last night. She sounded so upset when the stranger finally left. And there's no mystery any more; she's definitely using drugs again. Von's mouth tastes like garbage; it sometimes happens when he's stressed. This fog of murky memories keeps clouding up his brainwaves. The sight of that used syringe brought a sense of *deja vu*. The whole scene seemed familiar. But nothing's very clear now.

He's at a loss what to do; Charlene could be gone for hours. Stella's not well and she needs to see a doctor. Dressing her warmly, he carries her outside. Then he hovers for a moment on the fire-escape landing. What should he do now? How's he going to find a doctor? Techno pulses from the music store below them. Henry would know but the guy's a major dickhead. With Stella on his hip, Von reluctantly enters the store. Henry's kneeling on the floor beneath the new release rack.

'Hey!' Henry says, as Von walks in. Then, as if he's just remembered that they haven't been talking, his expression drops and he tries to tone things down a notch. 'Haven't seen you around lately.'

Von gives him a knowing look. 'Thought I'd stay out of your way for a bit.'

Henry laughs and twiddles with his dreadlocks. He doesn't appear to be holding any grudges.

'Listen, mate, I was a total idiot. Trust me, I've been thinking. What if one of my mates cracked on to my mum? Fair square, I'd want to flatten him.' Picking up a magazine, he whacks himself on the head. 'Don't worry, man. Your mama, my mama — they're strictly off limits.'

The guys shake hands. Stella shows her approval; holding out her tiny hands she tries to make a circle.

Von explains the reason for their visit. 'She's not been well — I need to find a doctor.'

Henry drops to his knees, starts checking out the Torturer. 'There's this lady down the road; she's pretty good, eh. Fixed me up a couple of times, seems to know what she's doing.' He grabs a post-it; scratches down an address.

As Von turns towards the door, Henry ruffles Stella's hair. Then he pulls out a bag from beneath the shop counter. 'Here, have these CDs — meant to give you them before. Salmonella Dub and Pitch Black. It's time you had a listen to some of our great Kiwi music.'

Crystal meth floods through Charlene's veins. The rush is so damned good she can conquer anything. Her mind feels sharp, her vision ultra clear. After checking on her kids, she'd left the apartment early and now, at last, everything's sorted. Kristie looked stunned when she turned up on her doorstep. But she was keen to help — she's always brilliant in a crisis. Just for tonight, she's going to take Stella. The girls have been close since they started at Endorphin. Kristie's not full-time, only works a couple of shifts; she's studying business at uni and the money comes in handy.

As Charlene ducks through a car park she's itching for a shower. She needs to scrub that bastard away, make a clean start of things. She's not convinced he'll stick to their deal. He promised her a month but what difference will it make? Without some kind of windfall, she'll never raise the money. Terrifying images start flashing through her mind. She sees Stella being kidnapped while she's working at Endorphin; Von getting injured when he tries to protect her. At least for tonight Stella will be safe. And tomorrow's her day off — she'll be home to keep an eye on things.

After sprinting down the alley, she quickly climbs the fire-escape. The door's slightly ajar; they'll need to find a way to lock it. She finds a note from Von — he's taken Stella to the doctor. Charlene heard her in the night when Von got up to help her. Her nose has been quite runny, but nothing really nasty.

Nearly an hour goes by before the kids get home. Charlene's still in the bathroom fussing with her make-up. Her eye is bloodshot, her cheekbone sore and swollen. She tried icing it with peas before smearing on some cover-up, but nothing can hide the mess of ugly bruises.

'How's Stella?' she asks, coming through to join them. She keeps her back to Von as she switches on the kettle.

'She's got glue ear, that's what the doctor reckons.'

Charlene spins around to face him. 'No way,' she responds. 'Stella always pulls her ears. Teething affects her that way — she's just been cutting a molar.'

Von's noticed her shiner. She can tell by his expression. His eyes avoid her face when he hands across some papers.

'The doctor was certain; she's written out a referral. A specialist will do tests and check out Stella's hearing. But she's going to need grommets.'

'Grommets?'

'Yeah, they're tiny tubes that fit inside her ear. They'll let in the air so her hearing should get better. Dr Jensen said that should help with Stella's talking.'

Charlene's restless, still charged with pseudo energy. In a way it makes perfect sense. That's why Stella doesn't say much — it must be hard to talk if you never hear the words right. Charlene can't help feeling guilty as she remembers all the times she got frustrated with her toddler. With Stella curled up on her knee, she quickly calls the specialist. But after five unpleasant minutes, she's starting to lose patience.

'This is my child,' she explodes. 'She's sick, she can't hear and your boss won't see her?'

'As I explained before, doctor will see Stella. But his first available space is not for five weeks. Is she taking antibiotics?'

Charlene tries to calm down before opening her mouth again. 'She has a script,' she says. 'We're going to get her started.'

'I'm sorry but that's the best we can do then. It's a very common problem; countless children are waiting for grommets.' The receptionist pauses to emphasise her point. 'Do you still want the appointment?'

'Yes,' Charlene answers. 'But you're a smug little bitch!'

'Excuse me? What did you say?'

'I said thank you and yes, I'll take the appointment.' Charlene notes the date after giving her name and details.

'She'll be right,' Von says when she puts down the phone. 'The doctor said she's not in too much pain.'

Charlene frets inside, totally unaware that she's digging away at herself. When the pain kicks in she glances at her hands, seeing the rash of ugly craters she's made with her fingernails. Aware that Von's looking, she dabs away the blood. His eyes move slowly upwards, settling on her face. Charlene hopes he's got the sense not to ask too many questions. When she stares him out, he quickly looks away again.

'Thanks for taking care of Stella; couldn't manage without you.'

Von doesn't respond; he silently holds his anger. Charlene sees through the charade as he pretends to read a magazine.

'I just wish we had more time,' she says. 'It's been crazy since you got here. Let me shout you lunch — just the two of us together. There's this great little café down at Lambton Quay.'

Von looks up, surprised. 'But what about Stella?'

As Charlene studies her little girl, she's filled with mixed emotions. Stella's not well; of course she needs her mother. But while Rob's out there, the kids aren't safe at the apartment.

'She'll be fine,' Charlene bluffs. 'I saw Kristie this morning — we work together at Endorphin. I'm going to drop your sister off; she's more than happy to have her.'

Stella appears to have built-in radar. She instinctively knows what her mother is saying. She starts clinging like a monkey to Charlene's tiny shoulder. Von sees the panic, the desperation, in his mother's troubled eyes.

'Look, I can tell you've had a shithouse night. But Stella's sick, I think she really needs you.'

Hugging her daughter, Charlene rocks her gently to her own internal music.

'Okay,' she relents. 'I just wanted to say thank you. You've come all this way, and you've been such a help with Stella.'

'But it's better if we all go. We'll rug her up; a bit of fresh air won't hurt her.'

Von carries the pram to the bottom of the fire-escape. Charlene follows him with Stella.

'She hasn't ridden in this for months. Always goes troppo when I buckle up the harness.' But Stella smiles and makes her mum a liar. She's happy to be strapped in; enjoys being a baby again. Charlene's heart races as she pushes her child down Cuba Street. She's so revved up she has to stop herself from running.

'What happened to your eye?' Von suddenly blurts out. 'Did that psycho bastard punch you?'

Charlene tries to stay cool. 'It was Rob,' she says, 'Pete's dodgy partner. But we've worked out a deal — he's nothing I can't handle.'

'Pete rang last night. But he was weird again, not making much sense really. He seemed to think there'd be some kind of trouble.'

A bit late, Charlene thinks. But at least he tried to warn her.

'Is he going to ring back?'

'Dunno,' Von says. 'I asked him to try later. He said to mention this word — sounded like 'kangaroo' — I reckon it's another of his crazy little codenames.'

Swallowing hard, Charlene masks her reaction. Pete's finally left a clue — now she knows where he's been hiding.

Jack parks his Cherokee beneath the jacaranda. He wants to clear his mail before he hits the surf at Leighton. There's a large soggy wad of uninvited junk mail. Without a second glance, it gets jettisoned into the garbage. Jack returns to the letterbox; finds the postcard from Te Papa. He chuckles to himself as he reads Von's sketchy message. He's tried to teach his son about their Moriori ancestors, but half the time he's convinced Von isn't listening. Jack gave him the brochures for Te Papa Tongarewa. But Von wasn't keen — he only packed them with reluctance. In a way Jack understands, it's a resistance he relates to. He certainly took his time before connecting with his ancestors.

It's been more than eighteen years since he left his home in Wellington. All this stuff is relatively new — this acknowledgement of their people. When Jack was growing up the Moriori weren't discussed — except as an example of some inferior type of human. He was even taught at school that his people were all gone. Jack spent his childhood years in a state of lost confusion. How can you belong to an extinct race of people?

Flopping down in the shade, he reads the postcard again. There's a tension behind the words; the boy's already having problems. Jack knows in his heart he shouldn't have let Von go. If he's honest with himself, it was the timing that really suited. He'd booked a break with some mates up at Gnarloo Station, and for the first time ever, his son wasn't going with him. For years they'd done the trip together, pitching a tent in the bush down near the ocean. Gnarloo is Jack's secret place, his little bit of heaven. But that last time away, he could see Von was bored. The boy's heart was back in Freo with Juice, the mates and footy. Watching his old man sailboard didn't hold the same appeal. Not when your girlfriend's drop-dead gorgeous and the party life is calling. Von moped around in silence and the whole thing was a downer. They finally packed the tent and left his heaven early.

Now he recalls the anguish of the last twelve months. It's been a shit of a year for Von; he's had a monumental struggle. At first he coped with the diabetes drama, but after Juice caught his eye, he didn't want to deal with it. He was thinking like a loser; thought he didn't measure up. Then he started to rebel, thought he'd skip a few injections — more than once that landed him in hospital. It was helping Juice at training that finally got him through. Von felt he had a purpose. She got him back on track again. But after the kids had a blue, they seemed to drift apart. Von was at an all time low and he just wanted to be out of there.

The night that Charlene phoned, Jack was working late at uni. By the time he got home, Von had already agreed to meet her.

'Dad, there's nothing for me here; Juice doesn't want to

know me. Charlene's my mum,' he tried to explain. 'It's a chance to get to know her.'

Jack knows he should have fought, told Von about their history. But when he spoke to Charlene later she sounded pretty stable. She was with a steady bloke; they had a little daughter. Did he really have the right to stop his son from seeing her?

As he pockets the postcard, Jack feels a little anxious. Before Von left, the boy made it very clear. He needed time out — Jack wasn't to harass him. But at times like this it's hard not to call. He knows Charlene and she's a proper bloody wild card.

They're sitting in Astoria down on Lambton Quay. It's a pretty swish set-up overlooking parklands. Stella's fast asleep, her face painted with spots of sunshine. Charlene's arm rests on the stroller as she browses through a menu.

'This is nice,' she announces. 'All of us, together.'

Von returns her smile but he can't help feeling wanky. Everything's so forced. He keeps wondering what she's up to. Now she's flirting with the waiter, ordering up big-time. There's a brittleness about her that reminds him of a twig — like it's only a matter of time before something's going to snap her. And it's strange, he thinks, as he studies Charlene's bruises. She's been trying to play things down since Rob roughed her up. But the guy wants his cash — there's no way he'll let it rest there. Nothing makes sense. And now she's spending all her money.

'Let's split it,' Von insists, pulling out his wallet. But Charlene acts offended and says she'll have none of it.

'It's my treat today; let's pretend it's your birthday! It always cut me up when I couldn't come and see you.'

He plays along with the pretence, but he can't buy her 'cut-up' story. Every birthday came and went and she never even called him. Dollars flash before his eyes. A seafood banquet fills their table. It looks and smells amazing but how can she afford it?

'Eat up,' Charlene insists. 'You know I want to spoil you.'

'After you,' Von replies, remembering his manners. But his mum just shakes her head and points a finger at the mussels.

'When you were small you loved chilli mussels. You could hardly walk or talk but you liked them really spicy!'

Soon he's up to his elbows in a feast of seafood heaven. The mussels are superb; then there's crayfish and prawns and a steak of blue bar mackerel. He's still scoffing down his fish when a giant cake arrives, a black forest torte with lashings of cream and cherries.

'You can't be serious,' he protests, already nearly bursting.

'I'll help,' Charlene says. 'Don't mind a bit of torte. I'm so glad,' she adds softly, 'that we got a chance to do this.'

'What d'you mean?' Von asks, worried by her tone.

'It's a mess,' she says, 'my life's a can of worms. If something happens to me, promise you'll get your sister out of here.'

Confused and anxious, Von challenges his mother. 'But you told me yourself — Rob's nothing you can't handle.'

'You're right,' she laughs, lighting up a cigarette. 'I've arranged to pay him back — just forget I ever said it.'

Von frets inside as they stroll back to the apartment. He's eaten too much, his stomach's turning over. He's reluctantly accepted that Stella's going to Kristie's. But he doesn't understand — he was happy to look after her. Charlene wouldn't budge; just shrugged away his offer. Instead, she suggested a couple of pubs. Said it was time Von got out and let his hair down a bit.

The night is a beauty; he decides to make the most of it. He might go for a wander then catch a movie later. Charlene's just dropped Stella at Kristie's, now she's taking a shower. Soon a rush of perfume floods the apartment. She always looks cool when she's going to Endorphin. But tonight, because of her bruises, she's overdone the make-up. Von's asked her what she does but she always answers vaguely. Once she play-slapped his face saying, 'I'm *not* a *stripper!*'

It always feels awkward when she heads off to work. He's sure there must be times when she doesn't want to go there. Each night before she leaves she gives Stella a hug, and then she turns to Von like she's not sure what to do. She hovers for a while. Nothing ever happens. Eventually she departs with a half-hearted 'See ya.' Tonight is no different; they go through their wobbly ritual. Her hand lingers on the door and she seems a little flaky. But then she turns around, comes back again and hugs him. It's a real hug this time, not one of those *what-do-I-do-now* hugs that she gave him at the airport.

'Thanks for everything,' she says. He finds he's hugging back. 'Really, I mean it. You're so much more than I ever imagined. A great son — special. Promise you'll go out and have a great night!'

The air is still thick with the smell of Charlene's perfume. With Stella not around, the flat feels so empty. There's an ache in Von's heart that he's finding hard to shift. For the first time since he came here, his mother showed she loved him. No strings were being pulled — that's how he knows it's real. And for some strange reason, he feels totally compelled to follow her.

The crystal's wearing off. Charlene feels a weight descending. Her neck's a painful knot of unresolved anxiety. Too late, she regrets how reckless she's been. It was fun indulging Von but she should have saved her money. The violence of last night still sits freshly in her mind. Her home's no longer safe; she doesn't want her family staying there. Running towards Endorphin, she feels a thousand eyes upon her.

Charlene's never felt this lost as she fights the pain of withdrawal. She'll need another point just to hold herself together. Rob knew who she was — she can't help wondering how he found her. Questions plague her now like a virus in her brain.

Was it Pete who let things slip?

Has he possibly betrayed her?

As she enters Endorphin, she tries to shake the paranoia. Pete's not that kind of man — he even rang to warn her. But she still feels afraid as she glances over her shoulder. Ever since she left for work, she's felt certain she's been followed.

Endorphin was easy to find; well lit and signposted. Von wanders past the bouncer, expecting an ID check. The guy doesn't raise an eyebrow. This is way too easy. After handing ten bucks to a pretty young lady, he heads to the bar and downs a couple of shooters. He keeps his head low — doesn't want Charlene to see him. But the silky warmth of vodka quickly does its job. Soon he's surfing a wave of frothy, smiling people. He's in the dark heart of the club, the pulsing aorta — the pump-pump-pump of the music is driving him along. He does a slow three-sixty degrees, soaking in the vibe. And then she's right in front of him — his frenetic, strobe-lit mother. For an instant she reminds him of a jewellery-box ballerina, all alone and twirling to her tinny wind-up music. Her eyes stare blankly but maybe it's the lighting. They belie the heated energy of her amazing, funked-up dancing.

All around Charlene, guys are staring up at her. Their heads drift together whispering secret things. The laughter is filthy when one of them gropes her leg. She loses her balance, nearly falls off the podium. Von shirt-fronts the bastard — tells him to keep his dirty paws off. Then his mother jumps down, starts whacking his face and screaming.

'Fuck off!' she yells. 'What the hell d'you think you're doing?'

She runs out of the club before he can answer. But there's not much he can say — he's not sure why he came here.

He tries to apologise as he chases her up the road. 'I'm sorry,' he yells. But she doesn't seem to hear him.

She's still brimming with pent-up rage when he enters the apartment. After a few awkward moments, Von tries to break the silence.

'I'm sorry,' he says again. 'But your act was really amazing.'

Charlene laughs weakly. He feels her anger cooling. 'I'm classically trained but who would ever know it? It wasn't my goal to end up dancing in a nightclub.'

And that's when he realises: he knows nothing about his mother. Von's head fills up with questions but he's terrified to ask them. But soon four words escape — there's no way he can stop them.

'Why did you leave?' He's waited ten long years to ask her.

Charlene looks defeated. She takes a while to answer. 'Jack asked me to go. I wasn't much of a mother.'

Gobsmacked by her words, he feels his chest tightening. There's no way that could be true. He's shocked that she would lie to him. But Charlene doesn't waver; her eyes are full of sadness.

'It was just for a while — wasn't meant to be forever. I was freaking out on drugs. Your dad got tired of rescuing me.' She takes Von's hand, stares at him intensely. 'You were so young; I was having trouble coping. For a six-year-old kid it wasn't a fit environment.'

'So Dad just kicked you out?'

'That's probably a bit harsh.' She's playing with her nails, no longer making eye contact. 'In a way it was mutual. Your dad heard about this doctor; he was running a program for people with addictions. His clinic was in Sydney — Jack insisted that I go. You were only six and I thought you should come with me. But your dad was adamant. He wouldn't take you out of school. So in the end we made a pact — I'd do the clinic on my own. I wasn't to come home until I'd sorted out my problem.'

Von feels angry, confused, pissed off with his father. Charlene stares into space, silently withdrawing. When he gently takes her hand, he's surprised by its coldness.

'Thanks,' he says, 'for being so honest. I always thought you'd run away. Dad never told me much so it helps to know the reasons.'

She squeezes Von's hand. 'Some things hurt too much to talk about. Now I'd better get back to work; Bill will be wondering what I'm up to.'

He kisses her goodbye; heads back to his bedroom. As he stares into the lava lamp, his eyes drift out of focus. He sees this swirling soup of lies that's been clogging up his life. She was gone for all those years, why didn't his father tell him? Jack banished her to Sydney — she could have been on a different planet.

She can hear Von snoring when she gets home at three. After making a cup of coffee she sits down at the table. Her sketchpad is waiting, she starts doodling with her pencil. Strokes move across the paper as she captures his expression; that look of disbelief when his troubled eyes met hers. She felt inadequate, exposed, up there on the podium. And she realises, too late, how badly she reacted.

A vision of her son emerges before her. She's playing with the image, trying to capture his true spirit. He's part Moriori — she often wonders what that means to him. His eyes revealed nothing when she handed him the shark's tooth. Jack was passionate about his people, but Von seems unexcited. It must be hard to connect, living so far from New Zealand. She often feels emotional when she thinks about that heritage — the Moriori were invaded then kept as slaves for decades. In a way she can relate, she's always fighting off invasion. She feels haunted by her past, enslaved to amphetamines. There's a collar around her neck as life drags her along.

Charlene puts down her pencil and studies her creation. She's proud of the way she's drawn the canoe; the expression on Von's face as he tries to control it. Sketching helps to clear her head — she needs more paper. Now a sudden gust of wind blows the front door open. She folds a sheet of cardboard, the last remnant of her sketchpad, and kneels on the floor as she tries to wedge the door shut. It's useless, she knows; wouldn't stop a cranky cockroach. But going through the process makes her feel a little safer.

With tired, heavy eyes, she pads through to Stella's tepee. She curls up in a ball on her toddler's tiny bed but she can't relax; every sound still makes her nervous. A sour metallic taste seeps into her consciousness. But she's totally unaware that she's gnawing her lips again.

He finds his mother's sketch lying on the table. Charlene's an artist, a talent, and she doesn't even know it. She's drawn him guiding a canoe across a vast, starlit ocean — a reef canoe like he saw at the museum. The morning isn't cold but Von begins to shiver. She's been out of his life for more than ten years yet she's visited the Chathams; there's all this interest in his people. In her own unusual way, was Charlene staying in touch with him?

Still stunned by the drawing his mind starts turning over. Wellington's like Fremantle with lots of arty people. If Charlene sold her portraits she might earn enough to give away the dancing. She's obviously got a gift; could even become famous. If she goes for this it would be better for everyone. Better for her; better for Stella, and easier for Von when he heads back home to Freo. He wouldn't have to spend every second worrying — wondering if the Torturer's okay and how they're both going.

He knocks on Charlene's door, eager to run things past her. Seconds slide into minutes and she still hasn't answered. He hears a muffled cry; it's coming from the tepee. Cocooned in

Stella's bed, Charlene's curled up like a foetus. Her mouth is smeared with blood when she turns around to face him.

'What happened?' Von asks, trying not to gag. 'Did that rotten bastard hurt you again?'

'It's the speed,' she explains. 'It sometimes makes me chew myself.'

This is definitely not the time to talk about a career change. There's terror in her eyes and he's not sure how to help her. The drugs are in control — Charlene's trapped in her own prison. Von often feels like that when he's shooting up his insulin. But he can't live without the stuff — his body doesn't make it. Charlene's addicted to amphetamines, filled with constant craving. She probably hates injecting speed. But without it she hates living.

'Mum,' he suggests, cautiously. 'We could all go back to Fremantle. You'd both be safer there and I could help you with this drug stuff.'

'Maybe,' she says, like she's actually considering it. Then she disappears into the bathroom, saying it's time she tidied up a bit. About ten minutes later, when she finally reappears, she's disguised her sores with a splash of bright red lipstick.

'I'm sorry,' she says. 'I have to collect Stella. But I'll think about what you said — we can talk about it later.'

Charlene rushes up to Stella when Kristie lets her in, but the toddler pulls away— she doesn't want to know her. Always the peacemaker, Kristie tries to smooth things over.

'Kids get funny when they're sick. She's still a bit under the weather.'

Charlene kneels down next to Stella, tries to win her over. 'Mummy loves you,' she says. 'I don't ever want to leave you.'

'Vonny,' Stella whispers, as she turns away again. 'Stella want Vonny!'

Hurt by the rejection, Charlene collapses into a chair. Kristie nervously plays with her dark, elfin crop. She wants to help; can see her friend is hurting.

'What if I worked some of your shifts, then you'd have more time with Stella.'

Paranoia gets the better of Charlene. She turns on her friend, snapping back defensively. 'So what are you suggesting? That I'm a crap kind of mother?'

Kristie knows the signs: the mood swings, the aggression. There's no doubt in her mind. Charlene must be using speed again. Instead of reacting, she manages to talk calmly.

'Von can't stay forever; there's no-one else to support you. Please let me help — it might ease the pressure a little.'

Charlene's struggling hard to hold herself together. 'You know what happened with Rob — I need to work those shifts. One way or another, I've got to raise that money.'

'Here,' Kristie says, pulling some notes from her purse. 'I know it's not much but it might make a difference.' Charlene hesitates for a moment before she takes the money.

'You should go and see the bank; it's really easy getting credit. If you speak to Bill, he's sure to give you a letter.'

For the first time in a while, Charlene starts to feel more hopeful. She's never thought about a loan. Kristie's always been a smart one.

'Thanks,' she tells her friend. Now she's sorry for being spiteful.

As Kristie folds her arms around her, Charlene can't help crying. 'Don't take my words to heart. I feel horrible for snapping.'

'You're forgiven,' Kristie says. 'And don't be a stranger. Stella's never any bother.'

He hears Stella's tiny feet climbing up the fire-escape. Pushing through the door, she runs across to meet him. She starts scaling him like a palm tree, her face all creased with dimples.

'Vonny!' she shouts, patting him fiercely on both cheeks.

She was only gone for one night but he's really glad to see her.

'I reckon someone missed you.' Charlene follows through the door. 'When I turned up at Kristie's she didn't want to know me.'

He's not sure what to say but it's cool that Stella likes him. He grabs his sister's hands, starts giving her a whirly. She laughs like crazy but soon her colour drains away. They flop down on the floor. Von can tell she's feeling seasick.

'Come to Mama?' Charlene urges. 'Is your tummy feeling funny?'

The Torturer frowns then runs off to her tepee. Charlene's face looks tense. Von can tell she feels embarrassed.

'I'm in the bad books,' she explains. 'She's been ignoring me all morning. Stella often gets in moods, especially when she's poorly.'

He's glad to have them home. It felt weird without their company. In a quiet, unspoken way, they're starting to feel like family. Now that Charlene's back, she might be ready to have a chat. There has to be a way they could all move back to Fremantle. Jack sent her away; he reckons his dad owes her. The least he could do is put them up till Charlene's better.

Von keeps worrying about Juice — he's ready to go home. They've been through a stormy patch and he needs to spend some time with her. He scribbled her a letter just before he left, trying to explain why he'd been acting like an idiot. Deep and meaningfuls aren't his thing; they always get him into trouble. It's always much easier working things out on paper. He must have said something right — she came straight round to see him. They found a patch of lawn, never bothered about the prickles, and all the fights, the misunderstandings seemed to vanish as they lay there. But he had to leave that night. He really hates not seeing her.

'You okay?' Charlene asks as she passes Von some nachos.

There's no way he's going to tell her that he's dreaming about his girlfriend. 'I'm cool,' he replies, trying to sound casual.

Charlene joins him on the couch. 'I feel better now,' she says, 'after that shaky start this morning.' But her lips still look tender beneath the smudgy lipstick. 'What you suggested earlier, about moving back to Freo. Well, it was kind of you to ask but it really won't be necessary.'

He stares at his mum; who does she think she's kidding. 'But the speed,' he says, 'you said it makes you hurt yourself.'

'I'd just woken up, you caught me by surprise. I know my mouth looked nasty but it's not exactly life threatening.' Her eyes keep darting about. She's obviously in denial.

'Whatever,' Von shrugs. He's not in the mood to argue.

'Don't be hurt,' she says gently. 'I'm going to get a bank loan. When I've paid off Pete's debt everything should be normal.'

When the phone starts to ring, Charlene rushes off to answer. After mumbling a few words, she hangs up very quickly.

'Bloody typical!' she snaps, as she plonks back down beside him. 'Bill's done it again; always forgets I've got a family. He wants me to dance tonight, but I hate working Sundays.'

'Just tell him you can't.' Seems like a simple enough solution. Charlene shoots Von a look like he's totally insane. He'll have to watch his words — he thought he was being helpful.

'Someone's called in sick. The dancers get the crowd going so I really need to be there.'

Von can tell his mum's exhausted. 'You should try and have a nap, I'll watch out for Stella.'

'Not today,' she says. 'I want to spend some time with her.' She looks wrung out, her eyes ringed with purplish shadows. Now she's buzzing about like a hornet in a bottle.

'What's up?' he asks. Something's obviously bothering her.

She finally stops fidgeting and sits down next to Stella. 'I don't like you kids being here alone when I'm working at Endorphin. Rob might turn up — what if he tries to hurt you?'

Just bring the bastard on, Von thinks secretly to himself. He's got a pretty good idea what the guy did to his mother.

'Take a look at me Mum: I'm six-five and growing! I'm more than capable of protecting Stella.'

Her expression is vague. Von's not sure he's convinced her.

'You're right,' she says eventually. 'I'm probably being a worrywart. And thanks,' she adds, 'for trying to make me feel better. You're twice the size of me. If there's any trouble, who am I kidding?'

Soon she's gone again, back to Endorphin. The Torturer's fast asleep — things should be nice and easy. He's tried kicking back with Henry's Kiwi music, but no matter what he does, Von can't shake the horrors. This knot of anxiety never eases up on him. Pete's dropped Charlene right in it; now people are abusing her. He hates what's going on. There must be something he can do for her.

Endorphin's packed. The crowd is tight and jerky. Charlene felt flat before the music even started. Her body aches with cramps, her nerves are really jumping. She's been powering on crystal for the last couple of days. It's either top-up again or wait for the avalanche. Glancing anxiously at her watch, she prays her break comes quickly. Her boss is in the crowd staring at her glumly. She tosses him a smile, instantly revs her moves up. Bill winks his approval as he's swallowed by some stompers. But as soon as he's gone, Charlene slackens off again. It's hard staying pumped when you'd rather be sleeping.

When her break finally comes, she heads for the back alley. But instead of shooting up in the toilets, she lights herself a cigarette. It's a freezing night and the chill gives her clarity. The pain's kicking in, but she's certain she can beat it. The exhaustion, the depression — they don't last forever, and she has to sharpen up if she's going to see the bank. She's got a steady income — Bill's writing her a letter. Charlene's confident now that she'll get herself a loan. Pete's safe for the moment but she knows he can't come home. If he did, he'd only get arrested. It's up to her to pay Rob off; that way her family can be safe again. But another nagging question won't leave her alone. Pete started up his scam to help them buy a home. He even showed her what he'd stashed, so what's he done with all that money? One night before he bolted, Pete made her sign a form. But she was running late for work and didn't have time to read it. Perhaps he made a risky investment? Things were different back then — she was naive enough to trust him.

There's a couple making love over by the wheelie bins. It's time to go inside. They could use a little privacy. She blows a couple of smoke rings as she walks towards Endorphin.

'Nice night,' a voice whispers from behind her, sending a spear of terror straight through Charlene's body. Pure adrenalin fuels her flight as she charges down the alley.

The damn phone is ringing again. What is it with bloody Kiwis?

'Hello,' Von snaps, half expecting the Seagull.

'Is Charlene there?' It's a new voice.

'Don't know,' he replies, not sure who is calling.

'It's Bill, her boss.'

'Oh,' Von says, surprised. 'She left ages ago; said she had to start early.'

'Are you her kid?'

'Yeah, I'm staying for a while.'

'Is your mother okay?' But Bill doesn't wait for an answer. 'It's just she didn't have her usual zip tonight. Then she took an early break and none of us can find her.'

Von's feeling nervous. He's not sure what to say. She could be sick from the drugs? Rob might have collared her? 'She's just tired,' he tells Bill, not sure if he can trust him. 'Mum works too hard, she gets exhausted.' He's aware of an edge creeping into his voice. 'She needs a break but she's desperate for the money.'

Bill doesn't answer straight away, but when he does it's nasty.

'Listen,' he snaps. 'Don't pull your sob stories on me. Charlene's a professional. All my girls get tired but they don't walk out on their shifts. When she turns up, doesn't matter what time, make sure she calls. If I don't hear from her tonight, she'll be out on her ear, right.'

Horrible scenarios start forming in Von's mind. What if Charlene's lying in some gutter, beaten up or overdosed? The Torturer's fast asleep but he's compelled to go and check on her. If his mother's in trouble, the next one could be Stella. He tries to calm down, plays some cruisy music. But it doesn't help — he's still beside himself with worry.

It's an hour since Bill called; Von can't stand it any longer. He decides to ring back — maybe Charlene's turned up again. Just as he's going to pick up the phone, he hears a huge clank outside on the fire-escape. Hopefully it's Charlene climbing up the stairs. He opens the door and steps into the darkness, but the only sign of life is a hungry looking tom-cat. A filthy storm is hammering down on Wellington — Von struggles to wedge the door shut against a wind that's fairly howling. After picking up the phone, he dials Endorphin's number.

'Charlene?' squeaks a girl when he asks about his mum. 'I haven't seen her for hours. Bill's going off his brain — he can't stand slackers.'

He's about to tell her to shut her mouth. But he realises, just in time, that won't get him anywhere.

'Mum's not a slacker; she's never missed a shift. You should check the toilets? She might have caught a virus.' A weird falsetto tone has hijacked his voice box.

'Settle down,' the girl tells him. 'I know your mum's not lazy. Bill's feeling touchy because he thinks she let him down. He just went to a lot of trouble writing her a reference. I'll go and check the loos — if she turns up, I'll call you.'

She hears frantic thumping, unaware that it's her heartbeat. Her eyes are blind. Wind is howling all around her. She tries to cry out, but all she hears is silence.

    An engine grunts into life. Charlene tastes the smell of diesel. Her lungs gulp in air as she's swallowed by unconsciousness. Dreaming now, colours swirl beneath her lids. In her mind she's a young girl torching petrol on a puddle.

There's nothing happening here. He can't stand it any longer. Von opens the door, steps onto the landing. Last night's storm has blown itself out but the redness of the sunrise suggests more wild winds are coming. As he stares into the sky, the clouds appear wounded; pink-tinged and bleeding from their fight with ugly weather.

He can't think, can't eat — he'll have to wake Stella. But the Torturer's not impressed when he goes through to rouse her. She pushes Von away, snuggles back beneath the covers.

'Get up,' he tries again. 'We're going to visit Mama.' But his sister's no fool. Her two-year-old eyes see through him. Von knows this isn't right but what else can he do? There's no way he can leave her. After dressing Stella warmly in her anorak and leggings, he sits her on his hip while he struggles with the door. She's starting to wake up — even seems a bit excited.

'Duck!' she says, as clear as a bell. Then she says it again as if he didn't hear her. Cowering on the landing is a battered pile of feathers. It's an enormous thing, a great lump of a bird. Von can't believe his eyes; he's sure this guy's an albatross.

They're spectacular birds, his dad's shown him heaps of photos — they're a symbol of peace in Moriori culture. But they're not the sort of thing you'd usually find on fire-escapes. This one's an orphan of the storm. The wind must have blown him here.

'It's an albatross, I think,' he tells his little sister.

'Duck, duck,' she corrects him, as she wriggles down ferociously. They crouch there together, watching the injured bird. His leg looks damaged; he's just clinging to consciousness. Von wants to stay and help, maybe take him to a shelter. But they've got to find Charlene — he can't wait here any longer. Stella fetches a doll from her weird punk collection and she lays it down gently beside the shaken creature.

'Good,' she says, smiling, as if that fixes everything.

But time is moving on. He'll have to distract her.

'Let's go,' he says. 'We've got to find your mama.'

She waves bye-bye to Duck as Von carries her down the fire-escape.

A couple of hours later they're sitting in McDonalds. Surrounded by warmth, it's a comforting place to hang in. Stella's painting milky patterns on the unwashed table. Von's at a loss what to do; he's searched the whole city centre. He started with Endorphin but the place was shut up tight. In the grey morning light it seemed bleak and rather sad — not the neon-lit dazzler he saw just over a night ago.

He bundles Stella up. It's time they headed home. He's trying to stay positive — Charlene might be back now. Then, just as they're about to turn up the alley, Von gets a brainwave: it's time to visit Henry. He's a guy about town — he could have seen their mother.

The store's just opened. Henry's sitting with a coffee.

'Yeah, I was there, man,' he says. 'Endorphin was really pumping. But I thought Charlene must've had the night off. I stayed until three but I never caught a glimpse of her.'

'Her boss rang last night. He reckons Mum took a break and she never came back. It's bizarre,' Von adds, 'I've just been trying to find her.'

'Bill's a bit of a bastard. I reckon he'd be a hard bloke to work for. I help promote his club, so he sends a few punters our way.' Henry flips through his teledex then passes Von a number. 'Give him a ring at home. Hopefully she turned up again.'

He's trying to act cool but Von can tell he's worried.

'Don't know what else to suggest, but your Mum's got friends. She could have spent the night with one.'

'Maybe,' Von agrees. 'This girl called Kristie — she helps out with my sister. I remember Mum saying she works at Endorphin.'

'Could be this edgy chick I've seen Charlene take her break with — all crazy knee-high boots and psychedelic tutus. She's tiny,' Henry adds. 'Like a funky little fairy.'

'But I'm sure if she stayed at Kristie's, she would've let me know.'

'Stay cool,' Henry says. 'If your mum's not back by tonight, I'll cruise down to the club — try and suss things out a bit.'

Duck, the albatross, is still huddled on the landing. Stella tries to get down, but this time Von won't let her. After plonking her on the couch, he switches on a kids' show. Then he picks up the phone and punches in Bill's number.

'Hello,' Bill rasps. His voice sounds truly horrible.

'G'day,' Von replies, feeling more than a little nervous. 'It's Charlene's son; you phoned me last night. Just wanted to make sure Mum finished her shift all right.'

'You've got a bloody cheek, ringing at this god-awful hour. No, she didn't come back and you can tell her straight from me — if she ever shows her black-eyed face around here, so help me …'

That's it, Von decides. The bastard's gone too far.

'Shut the fuck up and listen, man. Charlene works for you, right, and she never made it home. She's got a two-year-old kid and …'

But before he can finish the rotten jerk hangs up. Stella clings to Von's leg, her bottom lip quivering.

Jack clears his throat. It's still early in the morning.

'Sorry,' he says. 'I've just woken up. Is everything okay, son?'

'Mum's gone,' Von says, flatly. 'She didn't come home last night.'

Jack can hear the little girl grizzling in the background. 'Christ,' he says, alarmed. 'Would you like me to come over?'

Von takes a while to answer. 'No,' he says eventually. 'It's okay, I can handle it. She should be home soon — probably spent the night at a friend's place.'

Jack's worried about the toddler; he can still hear her whimpering. 'But your sister's only two. There's no way that she'll be coping.' Slamming his fist on the bedside table, he's shocked at the strength of his anger. She's bolted again. What the hell is Charlene playing at? 'Nothing's changed!' he snaps. 'Your mum's bloody irresponsible.'

Von responds with equal rage. 'Yeah, and you're so bloody perfect. It was you who sent her packing!'

'Watch your mouth,' Jack recoils, taken aback by Von's aggression. What in god's name has Charlene told him? 'I don't know,' he continues, 'what your mum's been saying. But she left to find a cure — it wasn't meant to be for forever.'

'She said you didn't want her back — not unless she kicked her habit.'

'She was a junkie,' Jack explodes. 'Charlene booked herself into a clinic because awful things were happening. It was a painful time,' he adds. 'Your mother knew how much she'd hurt you.'

'So you sent her away. Just like you did with Max, our dog you couldn't handle!'

Jack thinks back to those days. Some things Von won't remember. If Charlene needed a hit nothing else mattered. Far too many times she just took off and left him.

'You needed ten bloody stitches when that demented mutt got hold of you. And Charlene left you home alone with a kettle on the burner. I'm sorry to bring it up but you've got the scars to prove it.'

'That was my fault,' Von says. 'Mum told me not to touch it.'

'Son, you were only six. She shouldn't have left you in that position.' Charlene had taken off on a two-week rampage. When Von heard the whistle screaming he grabbed the boiling kettle, the red hot handle was in his hand before he felt it burning. Charlene didn't come home till their boy was out of hospital — she totally fell apart when she realised what had happened. Yes, he'd asked her to do the clinic but she was desperate to get things sorted.

'Dad, things are kind of crazy — I'm torn up by what's going on.'

'I know, son,' Jack replies. 'Sounds like the drugs have taken hold again. She could be gone for weeks — that's what happens on a bender. You can't deal with this alone, I'm coming over. But first I'll contact the police; they'll get you help for Stella.'

'No don't,' Von says. 'Dad promise, please don't call them.'

'Son, you have to think about your little sister's welfare.'

'I'm used to taking care of Stella and Mum should be home soon. She's a strange one,' Von adds, 'but you can't help liking her. She knows heaps about our people; she's even been to the Chathams.'

Incredible, Jack thinks. But in a way it doesn't surprise him. She always took an interest in his Moriori ancestry. 'Please don't think,' he says, 'that I'm saying she's a bad person.' Charlene's heart was huge — there was so much love between them.

'She's really been in the shit. This guy, Rob, Pete's partner, came around and bashed her.'

'Pete? That's her boyfriend?'

'Yeah, the cops are on his tail and his dealer mate's been after him.'

Jack pauses for a moment. This sounds bloody serious. 'Son, you need to be careful — I want to come over.'

'No, not yet,' Von argues. 'Dad, you said it yourself; Mum sometimes splits for ages. You'll be the first to know if there's any more trouble. Give me a week,' he insists, not waiting for an answer.

Jack despairs when he hears the empty dial tone. If the wheels fall off, he knows he'll be responsible. His son's on his own playing parent to a two year old. Charlene's caught up in some drama. It's a dangerous situation. As he climbs out of bed, his head spins in a panic. Von's half a world away — he wants to be there with him. Taking a long slow breath, he grabs the Yellow Pages. His son needs his help. He can't wait here feeling useless.

He feels a bit more hopeful after talking with his dad. Charlene's been on benders before; there's a chance she could be home soon. When Stella starts to yawn, he carries her to the tepee. She's missed a lot of sleep, probably needs to get more rest now.

Wandering outside, he goes to check on Duck. The poor guy's looking grim; Von wonders if he's hungry. He makes him up a meal of breadcrumbs mixed with water, then he scans the Yellow Pages for the local wild-life shelter. He calls a couple of times but doesn't get an answer. It's not too bad outside and the landing's pretty sunny. Not much else he can do. At least the albatross should be warm there.

When his sister wakes up, it's nearly six-thirty. She heads straight for the fridge — the Torturer must be starving. But as usual, there's no food; he'll have to buy some pizza. The sun has gone and it smells like it's been raining — they pass poor Duck shivering on the landing. He hasn't touched his bread: Von can see the bird needs help. As soon as they get back, he'll try and make a cosy nest for him.

The pizza place is warm and inviting. After waiting at the

counter, he orders a large ham and pineapple. As they climb into a booth next to the window, a stunning girl smiles over from her table. She's got a mane of jet-black hair that reminds him of Juice. The chick's eyes are huge grey almonds. She keeps staring like she knows him. Von's mind drifts away, wondering what Juice is up to. Athletics is her life, keeps her pretty busy, but it's hard not to stress when he thinks about her training. He used to be her running partner; that's how they got together. But there's always a queue of guys lining up to help her. He's been gone a long while and in his heart he trusts her, but Juice could have whoever she wants. He just hopes she isn't lonely.

Soon he's totally blown away by a reflection in the window. The raven-haired stunner is walking straight towards him.

'Can I join you?' she asks, not waiting for an answer. She plonks herself down on the bench next to Stella. 'I hate eating alone — could use a bit of company.'

The girl is drop-dead gorgeous. Von's feeling really awkward. Small talk's not his thing and he's not sure what to say to her. As if she reads his mind, she starts chatting away regardless.

'You're a cutie,' she tells the Torturer. Little Stella looks puzzled.

'She's my sister,' Von explains. 'She's two, her name is Stella.'

'I'm Riana,' the girl says, holding out her hand. But his paw's a sweaty mess — he wipes it dry before he shakes hers.

'Von,' he replies. 'It's really great to meet you.' An awkward silence follows. He's sure he sounded wanky.

'So,' Riana breaks the ice, 'are you giving your mum a holiday?'

He'd love to say *I do this full-time*. But Riana seems cool. She doesn't need to know his problems. 'That's right,' he says, instead. 'My mum's gone on a trip; it's just for a day or two.'

'Half your luck!' she says. 'You've got the place to yourself. I should bring my mates around, we could really run riot.'

Von forces a quick laugh, tries to share her joke. If the timing was right, it'd be cool to get to know her. But his heart's back home with Juice — nothing's going to happen here. The Torturer's getting fidgety. Soon she starts to grizzle. She reminds him of a leech the way she's clinging to his kneecap.

'What's wrong?' he asks, concerned. 'Are your ears hurting again?'

Riana's eyes were already big, now they look enormous. 'Poor kid,' she sympathises. 'Must be terrible having earache.'

'It's getting better,' Von explains as Stella clambers up his chest. He tries to calm her down as a guy serves up their pizza. But instead of eating, the Torturer's acting up. She snatches the salt, starts sprinkling it on the table.

'I'll head off,' Riana says. 'Looks like you've got your hands full.'

Stella grabs a slice of pizza and dumps it on the floor. Von takes a deep breath; his sister's crossed the line now.

'Stop it!' he yells, as she stamps it into the carpet. When he tries to pick her up, she screams uncontrollably.

Riana looks on disapprovingly. 'She's not well,' she says, upset. 'There's no need to be so tough on her.'

Great, Von thinks, as she heads for the door. The chick was seriously cool and he's just acted like a monster.

Henry's had no word from Von; he assumes Charlene's still missing. After locking up the shop, he stops by the apartment. There's a sick looking black-back trembling on the landing. Henry's always had a soft spot for the big, noisy gulls — he tries to cheer it up with a piece of tasty Kit-Kat. He knocks on the door a few times but nobody answers. In the end he gives up; it's time to get some dinner.

    Soon he's washing down his meal with an icy Lion Red. The crisp taste of beer, it works magic with green curry. Thai Panom's his favourite restaurant; he sometimes meets his friends here. But it's deserted tonight, no familiar faces. He wouldn't admit it to anyone, might tarnish his 'rock star' image, but after a day of non-stop music he's glad to have some peace and quiet.

    He checks his watch at nine — it's time to hit Endorphin. He never goes to clubs before eleven-thirty. Any earlier than that, there's not a lot of action. But tonight he's on a mission; he's hoping to find Kristie. If it turns out she's there, they might get a chance to talk before the club fills up with ravers.

    'G'day,' Bill says, greeting him at the door. 'Are you feeling all right? It's pretty early for you, mate!'

'Yeah,' Henry jokes. 'I was feeling a wee bit lonely. But seriously, eh, nothing's open on a Monday.' For a second he's tempted to ask about Charlene. But he pulls himself up, can't give too much away. Von would have been in touch if Bill had any news of her.

Henry passes Bill a twenty. Bill quickly hands it back again.

'It's on me,' he insists. 'You've been sending heaps of punters. And get yourself a drink — tell the girls it's my shout.'

Sitting quietly at the bar, Henry sips his Jack Daniels. He often waits like this for hours in the hope of seeing Charlene. It makes him feel like a school kid, he's got such a crazy crush on her. Now he watches as two dancers climb onto their podiums. He lets out a sigh, relieved that one is Kristie. Soon her body's moving rhythmically to the drum and bass music. She's a nasty little dancer, but nothing like Charlene. Charlene's a total drawcard — she's Endorphin's X-factor.

He ambles down to the dance floor, slides between some stompers and dances with some chicks at the base of Kristie's podium. If he stays here till her break he can easily catch her eye. Great planning, he thinks, as he grooves along to the music. Then, to his annoyance, he feels his bladder bursting. But if he has a quick leak now, he should be back before they finish.

When Henry returns, Kristie's not on her podium. It's strange, he decides, because the other girl's still up there. His eyes trawl the club and he spots her on the pillow seats. After buying another drink, he moves a little closer. He tries to listen in; she's deep in conversation. A guy's sitting very close with his arm around her shoulder, but her body language says it all — the funky fairy isn't happy. And that's when Henry realises — he's seen this freak before. He was hanging around Charlene. Henry's certain he's a dealer.

Bill's standing, arms crossed, in the middle of the dance floor. His foot taps in irritation — he can see the empty podium.

'Incredible,' he says, when Henry wanders up beside him. 'These chicks are all the same, completely unreliable. She's the second one this week who's done a bloody runner.'

'I know where she is. If you like, I'll go get her.' But when Henry turns around, the pillow seat is empty. 'That's weird,' he says to Bill. 'She was with a guy a second ago but she didn't look happy.'

'Domestics,' Bill snaps. His face contorts with anger. 'They should leave that stuff at home. Who needs them, bloody dancers!'

'She'll be back,' Henry says, wishing he believed that. When Bill heads to the bar, he decides to take a look around. People gather near the toilets if they've business to attend to, but the weather's caved in and the alleyway's deserted. He asks a chick he knows if she'll go and check the loos. But Henry finally admits defeat when she comes back empty-handed. Kristie's gone without a trace — he's left wondering what to make of it.

After salvaging some food they leave the pizza parlour. As their warm breath steams the air Stella gets excited. Her baby hands reach out, desperately try to catch it. Von's upset with himself for getting so annoyed. She's missing her mum and the poor kid's ears are hurting. He was six when Charlene vanished but the Torturer's so much younger. And she doesn't have the words to tell him what she's feeling. He gives her a hug when she snuggles into his shoulder. By the time they get home, she's fast asleep and snoring. Her tummy's full of wind, she's been farting like a trooper. Soon the air inside her tepee smells nothing like pizza!

Poor Duck has taken a turn for the worse. His eyes are like slits and he's dribbling brown vomit. He needs to come inside — Von starts searching for some blankets. Rifling through a shelf in the top of Charlene's wardrobe, he finds his mum's cosmetics stored messily in boxes. The second smaller wardrobe must belong to Pete: a rack of shirts, a couple of anoraks and a pair of muddy steel-caps. As he explores the upper shelves, a small scrap of paper feather-floats to the carpet. Curiosity wins, he picks it up and reads it — it's a lawyer's receipt made out to Charlene Taiaroa. He sits on his mother's bed, shocked by what he's reading. Charlene's buying a house in a place called Kaingaroa. The deposit was paid more than a month before he came here. She's not mucking about — it's a huge lump of money. Once again, he feels betrayed, hurt she didn't tell him. And what about Pete? Does he know she spent the money? Then, suddenly, Von remembers that last disturbing phone call. *When you see your mum, mention kangaroo.* He thought it was a trick — just another silly code name. But now it's all too clear, Pete was saying Kaingaroa.

He folds the receipt and sticks it in his pocket. The name has triggered something in his brain — a village called Kaingaroa that's on the Chatham Islands. Now it's all coming back, he's remembering what Jack told him. There was a skirmish on the beach when the first Englishmen came ashore — one of their Moriori ancestors was shot dead at Kaingaroa. But the Chathams are miles from anywhere. Why would Charlene make her home there?

His thoughts return to Duck still out on the landing. Grabbing Charlene's doona, Von makes a nest in front of the heater. When he gathers the albatross up, it offers no resistance. The poor bird looks worse in the brighter light of the apartment. His eyes are almost closed, starting to glaze over. Von hopes the warmth will help as he places Duck on the doona.

After nursing the injured bird, he unfolds the receipt again. If Charlene owned a place then why did she stay in Wellington? Especially with all the grief that Rob's been dishing out to her. The first time Pete phoned, he said

Charlene was full of secrets. He obviously knows her well. Von wonders what else she hasn't told him. If she's gone to the Chathams, it's unlikely she'll be back. But a house in Kaingaroa — something doesn't ring true there. As soon as he gets a chance, he'll have a chat with Henry. The guy's pretty street-wise; he's sure to have some theories.

The albatross stares with his dull, dying eyes. Then he burrows into the quilt and has another shiver.

Jack sighs in frustration as he shuts down his laptop. The earliest flight to Wellington doesn't leave till late tomorrow. At this time of year his workload is light, just fine-tuning units for first semester. His bags are packed; he could have been there by midnight. But he knows in his heart that Von won't be happy. The boy's got a stubborn streak, always likes to do things solo. He'd rather tough it out than accept his dad's help. But Jack can't stay home while Von's in this crisis.

It's more than sixteen years since Jack's been home to Wellington. Last time he flew across was for his father's funeral. Now he picks up a photo from the shelf above his desk. He sees Mary, his mother, a proud Ngati Mutunga Maori and his unassuming father Riwai, who rarely spoke about his ancestry. They both look very young, most probably in their twenties, and the strength of their love shines out from the photo. But there's sadness there too; Jack often had to witness it. Mary's tongue was sharp and she used it to hurt Riwai. When he talked about his ancestors, she always shut him down. She made him out to be a fool, kept denying he was Moriori.

'The Moriori are gone.' It was Mary's favourite argument. *'Stop living in the past, they were wiped out by diseases. Get over it, Riwai — you're just another Chatham Islander.'*

Jack hasn't seen Mary since they fought at Riwai's funeral. But he knows she's still there at the family home in Wellington. In the years before his death, Riwai embraced his special heritage. He finally pushed aside his shame and felt proud of being Moriori. A renaissance was underway; history was being rewritten. The old man was excited — Jack could sense it in his letters. At last his people were being acknowledged for who they were: the original inhabitants of Rekohu and Rangiauria, the misty Chatham Islands. But sadly for Riwai, Mary couldn't share his joy. She argued that more than one event had impacted badly on the Moriori. In many ways she was right. When English sealers came to Rekohu in the early eighteen hundreds, they ravaged the seal colony — a vital source of food and clothing. And after European settlement, over fifteen hundred Moriori succumbed to foreign diseases. But Mary couldn't accept that terrible things had been kept hidden. Brutal massacres, years of slavery; secrets buried in the sand — the lethal legacy of her ancestors, the awful aftermath of invasion. It all happened long ago and her great-grandfather had played his part in it. The Ngati Mutunga and Ngati Tama wreaked havoc on Riwai's people. Mary didn't want to know. Some things were best forgotten.

Jack aches with regret when he thinks about his mother. She's an old woman now; there shouldn't be this rift between them. He feels her shadow on his soul; Mary's still a vital part of him. So why, he wonders, is it so hard to forgive her? For most of his adult life he's had no contact with his parents. And, Jack realises now, Von's life is not much different. He's grown up without a mother — his whole world's been built on secrets. Jack always thought it kinder to protect him from the truth. Why spoil a few good memories by painting ugly pictures? But now he starts to wonder — was it Von he was protecting? If Jack's honest with himself, he hates looking back. Charlene's life was out of control — intervention had to happen. But his memories are murky, like a bad dream long forgotten. Did he ask her to try the clinic? Or did he push his wife so hard she thought she had no option?

Stella's bailed up in her tepee, frightened out of her brain. Someone's hammering on the door but there's no way Von can answer. He's too busy trying to catch an albatross Duck's risen from the dead — he's demolishing the apartment. Charlene's porcelain ballerina lies in pieces on the floor; a splat of poo is sprayed across the carpet. Von dives for the door, dislodging the wedge as a gush of icy air pours through the doorway. The albatross smells freedom but gets himself tangled. Now he's perched on a woman's chest, pinning her to the landing. Duck clings, quite determinedly, to his final rocky outcrop. The woman seems remarkably calm, considering her predicament.

'Get it off,' she requests politely. Von's not sure what to do. The whole scene's totally crazy — a bird's hanging off her bosoms. If he tries to lift Duck off, he might accidentally touch them. Instead he grabs some bread and coaxes the bird towards the railing. Duck's appetite is back, the bread works like magic. In a sudden spread of wings, their feathered friend is gone.

'Duck!' the Torturer screams. 'Stella want my Duck back.'

'But he's better,' Von tells her. 'He's gone to find his babies.'

She drops her bottom lip and toddles back inside, closely

followed by the mysterious knocking woman.

'Jenny Watts,' she introduces herself, 'from the Department of Child, Youth and Family Services.'

'Von Taiaroa,' he replies, matching her formality, 'from Fremantle, Western Australia.'

Welfare Jenny's voice is cold. 'There's no need to be facetious.' She looks Von up and down, shakes her head before continuing. 'Does Charlene Taiaroa live here?'

'Of course, she's our mother.'

'Oh,' says the woman. 'Well, it would be helpful if you fetched her.' As she speaks, her eyes are studying Stella. 'It's very important. I really need to talk to her.'

'She's not home,' Von explains. 'Can I give her a message?'

Jenny doesn't answer; she starts sniffing around the apartment. 'We got a call,' she announces, 'informing the department that your mother is away.'

His dad threatened to call the police; Von wouldn't put it past him.

Jenny's nosiness escalates. She discovers Stella's tepee. 'Is this where the child sleeps?'

Von reluctantly nods his head.

'There's bird excrement all through her bedding. I'm sorry,' she says. 'But this is a health issue now. I'll need to file an official report.'

'But you saw the albatross; he's the one who made the mess. I only brought him in because I thought he wouldn't survive. Stella loved him,' Von explains. 'It would have killed her if he'd carked it.'

'I'm sure no harm was intended.' Jenny's attitude starts to soften. 'But Stella's welfare is at risk — we do have strict guidelines.' She starts moving towards the door. 'I'll be back,' she adds, 'to make arrangements for your sister.' As he watches the woman leave, Von knows he's really blown it.

He tries to calm down. He's got to hold this thing together. When Jenny Watts returns she'll probably take Stella. But this is his sister, his blood; he's the only one who's left for her. They've got to get away; it's not safe here any longer. Anger and confusion wrestle in his mind. Things weren't perfect but he's sure Charlene loved Stella. That's why it's so hard to accept that their mother would abandon her. Remembering the ancient shark's tooth, Von goes through to his cubby. He stares at the fossil and its simple arcane beauty. Folding it in his palm, he absorbs its ancient energy — Charlene found it on the islands; it's like a special link between them. The shark's tooth was her gift — *a little piece of your homeland* — she seemed so happy when she spoke about the Chathams. And now, it would appear, she's bought herself a house there. He's got a feeling in his gut that's where they're going to find her.

The Torturer's being difficult; she's refusing to cooperate. When he sits her in her pram she goes stiff as a cadaver. One minute she's the toddler from hell, the next she's sobbing and clinging like a baby. Nothing else for him to do, he's going to have to carry her. He heads straight for the mall where he's seen a student travel shop. As they approach the glassy shopfront, Stella spots her own reflection. He's waving madly at the window when a girl inside starts laughing — she's a tall, athletic beauty with a mop of fiery tresses.

'That was sweet,' she says, after opening the door for them. Her name tag, which says Keira, sits alarmingly close to her cleavage. 'It's great to see a pair of happy faces.'

He feels like a tool. Knows he must have looked ridiculous. Seems the way to Keira's heart is to make a total twit of yourself.

'Okay,' she says, as Von sits down at the counter. 'What can I do to help you?'

But before he can answer, Stella starts to whimper. She climbs onto his knee then spews all over his t-shirt. Keira grimaces as she goes to fetch some tissues.

'I'm the oldest of six.' She kindly wipes the chuck off. 'I know what it's like — I'm always bloody babysitting.'

Cradled in Von's arms, Stella seems to be okay now.

'Thanks,' he says, embarrassed, as Keira bins a mountain of tissues.

'Right,' she tries again. 'Where were we before the chuck-up?'

'We need to fly to the Chathams; the first flight available.'

She looks at him strangely. 'Is the little one your daughter? You seem young to be a parent.'

He has to think quickly. 'I'm taking care of my sister while our mum's away on business. But she's going to join us later.'

Keira seems convinced. 'Cool,' she says and starts tapping on her computer. 'I've got seats on a flight tomorrow afternoon. But you'll need accommodation before the airline takes your booking.'

If Charlene's in Kaingaroa, they won't need a place to stay. But there's still a huge chance they won't find her on the islands.

'What d'you reckon?' Von asks. 'Just a cheap place should do.'

'The Roos Roost is okay. It's a backpackers' lodge — good value for students.'

Keira rings up straight away to check availability. 'How long?' she mouths, as she makes the reservation.

'Not long,' Von says. 'Reckon a week should probably do it.'

Henry's in the storeroom sorting out his stock. It's been a big day; the new releases need replenishing. The door alarm buzzes while he's sifting through CDs and he finds Von and Stella standing at the counter. Henry's not surprised; thought he might have seen them sooner. Von's eyes are ringed with shadows. Stella's hanging off his shoulder.

'Hey, man,' Henry says, trying to keep things cheerful. 'I've been thinking about you guys — any word about your mother?'

'Just weird stuff,' Von replies. 'I'll fill you in later. But seriously, mate; we've been dropped in the shit. Someone dobbed Mum in to Welfare and they're coming back for Stella.'

'That's stink,' Henry says as he dashes out the back. He returns with a shabby mattress and dumps it on the carpet. 'This is home away from home, right. I kip here myself when I've had a big night, eh.'

Shaking his head, Von looks a bit frustrated. 'Mate, no-one's moving in. We're flying to the Chathams.'

'The Chathams?'

'Yeah, something's come to light. I reckon Charlene's over there.'

Strange, Henry thinks. He hopes Von knows what he's doing. 'Leave your sister here while you go and grab your gear. If Welfare's on your case, you can't wait till tomorrow. I'll close up early then we'll head straight back to my place.'

Henry's got to tell the kid what he saw at Endorphin, but not here, he decides — Von looks too strung out to listen.

While Henry's watching Stella, Von rushes to the apartment. He's relieved Welfare Jenny isn't waiting on the landing. He gathers a bunch of Stella's clothes but most of them are grubby. At least they'll keep her warm — that's all that really matters. Now his insulin kit is packed and the Torturer's earache medicine. Remembering Charlene's omen, he picks up his shark's tooth. *Something that old has to be lucky* — luck's certainly one thing they could use an extra dose of. After pocketing the tooth, he throws on his backpack. Von pulls the door shut; he can't get away quick enough.

Henry locks the store and they pile into the Camira. Von fights back paranoia as he checks the rearview mirror. What if Jenny Watts is spying? She might have seen him leave the apartment. But Henry stays cool; tries to reassure him.

'Relax, man, it's never goin' to happen.'

But Von won't feel relaxed till they're safely on the Chathams.

Henry lives alone in a one bedroom cottage. He's being a real mate, even shouted a couple of pizzas. It's been a long day and they could all use some sleep. After finding a few spare rugs, Henry tries to make things comfy.

'Sorry, I've got no extra beds — I hope you guys can get some shut-eye.'

The Torturer dozes off on a small velvet couch. She's been a bit quiet since she chucked up at the travel shop. Von grabs a book from his backpack then flops into a beanbag.

About ten minutes later, Henry wanders in from the kitchen. 'All this shit's going through my brain.' He's made them both a Milo. 'There's no way I'm going to sleep, man.'

Von can relate. His mind's a maze of questions. He's worried sick about Charlene and what to do with Stella. And he's been filled with strange emotions since booking their flight to the islands. Jack calls Chatham Island — Rekohu — the Moriori name for it. He gave Von the book he's only just been reading. Tonight, as he browsed through it, a deep sadness grew inside him. The invasion, the slavery, all that suffering on Rekohu — what's it going to feel like when he finally gets to land there?

'Good book?' Henry asks.

'It's a present from my dad — all this stuff about the Moriori.'

Henry laughs and shakes his head. 'Most kids get money or games for their X-box.'

'Too right,' Von agrees. 'But my father's a historian!'

'Weird,' Henry says, 'but in a cool kind of way.' At first Von thinks he's joking but Henry's face is serious. 'Yeah, someone like me, I could have used a few good books. I was hopeless at school, half the time I wasn't listening. And I swear to you, mate, I know nothing about your people.'

Lying on her back, Stella starts to cough. Von puts one hand under her shoulder and gently rolls her over.

'Listen,' Henry says, once Stella settles down. 'We really need to talk; I'd like to run a few things past you.'

'Sure,' Von says. His mate is looking serious.

'No disrespect intended but Charlene isn't on the Chathams. Just think about it, man. She disappears into thin air; no-one hears a peep from her. But she's not that kind of person — she wouldn't do that to you guys.'

Henry's completely in the dark. There's stuff Von needs to tell him. But before he can gather his thoughts, Henry's chatting again.

'Last night I called by Endorphin, thought I'd have a talk to Kristie. But this punter was bothering her; I'm convinced the guy's a dealer. I've seen him around your mum — he's a seriously dodgy camper. I tried to find Kristie later, but the chick had totally vanished. Mate, history's repeating — something suss is going down here.'

Von's gut tells him Henry's right. Something suss is going down. Maybe the dealer bothering Kristie was Pete's pissed-off partner. Charlene hinted at the restaurant that more bad stuff could happen. If she's hiding from Rob, he may suspect that Kristie's sheltering her. What if he's kidnapped both the women? And if that's the case, are they prisoners here in Wellington? Von's head swims with possibilities but it's all just speculation — he still can't shake this feeling that Charlene's gone to Rekohu. After digging around in his pocket, he hands the receipt over.

Henry seems a bit perplexed. His brow furrows as he reads it.

'She's buying a place. But where is Kaingaroa?'

'Kaingaroa's a village, and it's on the Chatham Islands.'

'But you're talking eight hundred kilometres east of New Zealand. No way,' Henry says. 'That's too weird to contemplate.'

A troubling thought starts forming in Von's brain. Charlene left them both behind — there hasn't been any contact. If his theory is right and she's over on the Chathams, there's a very real chance she may not want to see them.

He stares at Henry now. It's time he filled him in a bit. 'Mum's boyfriend's a crook; hell, her life's in total chaos. I guess you wouldn't know; she's had big problems with amphetamines. I called my dad when she first disappeared — she's done this before, used to bolt when I was small. Dad's convinced she's on a bender.'

'People change,' Henry says, not buying the bender theory. 'I've seen Charlene with Stella — she wouldn't take off and leave her.'

'Mum's stressed,' Von argues, 'and I know she's using speed again.' But deep in his heart he agrees with Henry. Things were different when he was small, the drugs were in control but she'd sorted herself out before this shit with Pete happened. 'Mum was clean for years until her nerves got shot to pieces. She would have given up, she felt bad about using.'

'And her boyfriend's a crook?'

'Yeah, he was cooking all this crystal. Then he robbed a service station because he owed his partner money. One night, after work, Mum brought a stranger home. It was really late, I didn't get to see him but the walls are pretty thin — I heard the bastard laying into her. Turns out it was Rob, Pete's drug dealing partner.'

'Shit,' Henry says.

Von's mind turns to mud when he thinks about that night. 'It was terrible,' he says. 'I wanted to help Mum but I had to protect my sister. This guy was a maniac, I was scared he'd really hurt her.' Von squirms with discomfort, feeling like a coward. He's taken aback when Henry gives his vote of confidence.

'What a choice,' he says, 'but Stella's just a baby. A psycho like that, who knows what he'd be capable of.'

Yeah, Von thinks, wondering what else Rob's been up to. 'Pete called the same night but Mum was still at work. He left this weird message, said to mention Kaingaroa. They'd spent time on the Chathams — that's why I'm sure she's gone there.'

Henry stares at the receipt while he twiddles with his dreadlocks. 'Maybe,' he says, thoughtfully, 'but something definitely doesn't add up here. She never told you about this place?'

'Not a word,' Von says. 'I was hunting for a blanket when the receipt fell out of Pete's wardrobe — that's the first I ever heard of it.'

'Mate, I think I've worked things out.' Henry's looking very smug. 'This house in Kaingaroa — I reckon your mum's in the dark. I wouldn't mind betting she knew sweet-fuck-all about it. Pete probably bought the place so he'd have a little getaway; maybe he put it in Charlene's name because he's got a criminal record.'

Interesting theory but Henry's only guessing. 'Then why would he ask me to mention Kaingaroa?'

'Your mum's been to the Chathams, she'd know about Kaingaroa. He's found a safe base, that's his way of trying to tell her. We could argue the point all night, but it's not a wise move to take off with your sister.'

Von hates to admit it but Henry's making sense. Flying to the Chathams — the whole thing scares him shitless. But Welfare's after Stella and he can't risk staying in Wellington. Not when there's a chance that Charlene might be over there.

'There's something else,' Henry says. 'What if we're wrong about the bender? Charlene could turn up at the apartment and find both her kids have vanished.'

'I hear you,' Von says. 'Mate, I know my plan sounds crazy. And if my brain was thinking logically, I'd be the first to agree with you. But it's not just the receipt — there's this chain around my heart. Something's dragging me to those islands; I'm convinced that's where I'll find her.'

It's a typically gusty day and the turbulence is fierce; Jack admires the pilot's skill as they surf a wave of wind gusts. Now his heart skips a beat. The plane's approaching Wellington. Lush, forested mountains spring up from the ocean. Brightly coloured villas perch on every hillside. Jack's moved by the beauty as they fly across the harbour. There's a sudden noisy clunk — the wheels are dropping down. A few jarring bumps later, the plane's safely on the runway. He lets out a sigh, relieved to be home. In less than an hour, he hopes to see his son again.

Quickly claiming his suitcase, he makes his way through Customs. A hire car is waiting and he heads straight for the city. Much of Wellington seems unchanged; the streets still look familiar. In just ten minutes he's at the rougher end of Cuba Street. There's a two-storey building at the address that Charlene gave him. It's old, almost derelict; probably late nineteenth-century. Jack parks his car, starts searching for the apartment. He eventually tracks it down at the rear end of an alley. Climbing the rickety fire-escape, he prays Von won't reject him. He reaches the landing, stops to take a breather. Then, just as he's about to knock, Jack hears footsteps below him.

Henry usually opens the shop but he's decided to chuck a sickie.

'You've been great,' Von says as they're driving to the airport. 'The man in a crisis.'

'It's nothing.' Henry says. He looks a bit embarrassed. 'You're a family, right — we've got to keep you guys together.'

They pull into a bay outside the airport terminal. Henry gives Stella a wink before shaking Von's hand fiercely. They stand there on the pavement. Von feels a little awkward. Henry's so intense — it's like he doesn't want to leave them.

'Is there some way I can find you if Charlene turns up?'

'Yeah, I've booked a room at the Roos Roost backpackers'. I don't have their number but you'll find it on the internet.'

'Right,' Henry says. 'You'd better get going. But as soon as you're back, make sure you come and see me.'

After Henry says goodbye, Von takes his sister's hand. Official looking people patrol around the airport. Every time they look his way, he starts panicking about Welfare. Picking Stella up, he checks in at the desk. It's surprising all the stress hasn't given him a hypo — he won't be much use if he ends up in a coma.

They wait for their call in the busy airport cafe. While Stella's scoffing down her chips, Von gives himself a thumb stab. It's a nasty little procedure, testing blood sugar levels. But his reading's still okay, well within the normal range; being strict with the injections must have kept him out of trouble. Stella holds out her thumb as he's packing his kit away. The kid really cracks him up — she's waiting for her blood test.

'It hurts,' he tries to explain. Her little face turns glum. Stella thinks she's missing out but there's no way she gets a thumb stab.

Soon they're walking towards the plane, hand in hand across the tarmac. As Stella tugs on his arm, she looks incredibly fragile — like a little lost waif on a quest to find her mother. Von asks himself, yet again, why is he doing this? Charlene might have gone to the Chathams so she doesn't have to be with them. Stella needs her badly — that much is obvious. But this nothingness in his heart, does he need his mother too? He often aches to see Charlene but it's so hard to admit it. Why can't he just stop loving her, find some way to let her go? Because he's clinging to that moment not long before she vanished — that split second when they hugged; he felt sure she loved him too. But what if he's got it wrong? He's not that good at reading things.

Now take-off's been delayed; there's some malfunction in the propellers. It's a dinosaur of a plane — a fifty-year-old Fokker. A team of anxious technicians dash about with screwdrivers. The guys look totally freaked which doesn't instil a lot of confidence. It's an incredibly long trip between Wellington and the Chathams. If the plane conks out, they're straight into the ocean. At last the engines scream into life; the whole aircraft is vibrating. Soon a round, friendly hostess starts dishing out boiled lollies. Unlike the technicians, she looks incredibly calm. When Stella starts to whimper, she helps her with her seat belt.

'It's a silly old plane,' she jokes. 'But there's nothing to get upset about.'

The Fokker roars up the runway. Von's convinced they'll never make it. As he listens to the spiel on emergency procedures, he can feel it in his gut — this flight they're going to need them.

Jack glances down the stairs, expecting to see Von. But there's a smartly dressed woman and a uniformed police officer. As they quickly introduce themselves, Jack's not sure what to make of things.

'Jenny Watts,' the woman explains, 'Child, Youth and Family Services.'

He nods his recognition. They've spoken on the phone. When he first called the police, they referred him to Jenny.

'And this is Constable Grey. He's organised a search warrant.'

'Search warrant?'

'Yes, I called by yesterday, just to check things were okay. Von said Charlene was out but I'm certain he was covering. It's like a mad-house in there; the living conditions are terrible.'

'I'm confused,' Jack admits. 'Can you explain about the warrant?'

Aware of the time, Jenny tries to keep things brief. 'Stella, the two year old, needs to be in care. I called around this morning but your son wouldn't answer. The door has no lock, as I'm sure you've probably noticed, but I can't go inside without this piece of paper.'

'Ready?' the constable asks.

Jenny nods her confirmation. The door swings open to a world that Jack's forgotten. Charlene's painting of Fremantle Harbour is the first thing that greets him. The apartment smells atrocious. It looks like it's been ransacked. Jenny shows Jack the mess in Stella's tepee bedroom. He can't help gagging when she pulls back the doona.

'Bird shit,' she explains. 'They had a pet called Duck — Von said it was an albatross.'

'No way,' Jack says, surprised. 'They're enormous great birds and they don't hang out in Wellington.'

'Von's not the first newcomer to mistake a black-back for an albatross. Your son's got a good heart — he was doing his best for Stella. But he showed a bit of attitude. You can see for yourself, this is not a fit environment.'

Leaving Jenny alone to complete her report, Jack takes a peek in Von's makeshift bedroom. There's a portrait of his son taped above the camp bed, a pencil sketch, and the style is unmistakable. Charlene's drawn their young son as a proud Moriori. Jack's touched by her insight and the detail in the drawing. And he can't help smiling at the turquoise blue Transformer quilt. They were Von's favourite toys — he's surprised that she remembered. Pulling the chest drawer open he spots a travel diary. A present from one of Von's teachers, he doesn't expect to find much in it. Sitting down on the bed, Jack flips through the empty pages. He finds a solitary entry dated only yesterday:

She's got this great dirty laugh, my mum. Just bursts right out in the worst possible places. And sometimes, when the joke is extra filthy, her eyes expand; her mop of dark blond hair flies back, then this obscene cackle erupts from deep inside her. It hurts to think she'd leave when I've only just got to know her. But I can't forget that moment when she showed how much she loved me. Which is why, I suppose, after everything that's happened, there's an ache in my heart — I know I've got to find her ...

Jack fights back tears as he reads Von's words. It's obvious to him now — the kids have quit the apartment.

'In here,' Jenny shouts, calling from Charlene's bedroom. She points at a used syringe that's lying on the carpet.

'It's probably Von's,' Jack says. 'My son's a diabetic.' As the words pour out, he knows he's talking rubbish. Von would never leave used gear lying on the carpet. It's obviously Charlene's. Now Jack's wondering why he lied for her.

'Kids,' he adds. 'They're bloody hopeless with their garbage.'

Jenny looks at him doubtfully. 'Charlene used to have a habit ...'

Jack stares at the syringe. He wants this conversation ended. 'And as I said, Von has diabetes.'

An awkward silence stretches out between them; it lingers in the room like an unanswered question. Jenny clears her throat, tries to get back to business.

'Mr Taiaroa, a few weeks ago we received an anonymous report. A friend of your wife's was worried about the toddler. She was afraid Charlene was leaving her alone at night. But

Stella seemed well adjusted when I called around to see them. And Charlene was very honest — she explained they'd had a rough patch. She said a member of her family was coming to help with Stella. I felt convinced that she had her act together.'

Aware his palms are sweating, Jack's disturbed by what he's hearing. Charlene vanished from Von's life for over ten years. Did she only get in touch because she wanted something from him? As he quietly fumes inside, Jack wonders what Von's feeling. Was this whole reunion a lie? Did Charlene deceive him?

They've been soaring above the Pacific for almost two hours. Stella's dozed on and off but now she's getting restless. Von stares out the window at a mountain range of clouds. Now the plane goes into descent revealing a turquoise ocean. On the hazy horizon, something is emerging. A puff of pale smoke slowly grows into a land mass. His eyes fill up as he studies the misty island. Swallowing hard, he tries to rein in what he's feeling. This thin thread of hope is anchored to his soul — it's just pulled him to this place like a piece of ancient driftwood. Stella reaches up and harvests a tear. She pops it in her mouth, dissolving Von's emotions.

Closer now, he sees long, white beaches. An albatross glides below him, soaring towards the breakers. It looks haunting, luminous against the backdrop of the sea. Stella reaches out, starts scratching at Von's neck. Her ears must be hurting with the sudden change in pressure. The hostie's there in a flash, eager to help the Torturer.

'It's her ears,' he explains. 'Not used to the pressure.'

After Stella has a drink she seems a little better. Her crying soon subsides and she sucks her thumb ferociously.

As they soar across a bay, he can see a coastal township.

'Waitangi,' the hostess says. 'The pilot's doing a fly-by. Sam, one of the islanders, passed away in Wellington. That's his home over there — most of our passengers are mourners. It's sort of a last farewell before the funeral.'

A few minutes later, the intercom starts crackling.

'Welcome,' the pilot says. 'Thanks for flying Air Chatham. It's a pleasant twelve degrees at the moment in Waitangi. I hope you enjoy your stay on the wonderful Chatham Islands.'

They're the only ones left at the tiny airport terminal. All the other passengers had people to meet them. Von's not sure what to do; they need to find the Roos Roost — but there's no transport around, not even a taxi. To make matters worse, Stella needs the toilet. He helps her onto the loo, sits with her for ages, but it's just a false alarm. Now the Torturer says she's thirsty. While he's searching through his backpack for one of her drinks, he can't help noticing a woman who is watching them. Handing Stella her juice, he tries to act casual. The woman's still there, not far behind them. She catches Von's eye — starts waving at him madly.

'Kia ora,' she calls out, in a bright, friendly voice. 'How are you?'

'Hi,' he answers nervously. 'To be honest, we're kind of stuck here.'

The woman's probably in her fifties. She's got a round, tanned face that's seen a lot of weather. Her eyes draw Von in. Something tells him she's part-Maori.

'You've flown to the Chathams and there's no-one here to

meet you?' She's obviously amused. Von feels a bit self-conscious.

'That's right,' he says. 'Didn't know that was unusual.'

The woman studies him for a moment like she's making some decision. Von's being measured up. She's not sure what to make of him.

'Ahinata,' she says eventually, holding out her hand. 'There's no-one else around — guess it's up to me to help you.'

Soon they're speeding towards Waitangi in the woman's old Cockroach. It's an ancient four-wheel drive with worn-out suspension. The road is unsealed which makes for bumpy driving.

Ahinata starts a chat in the rearview mirror. 'I had freight to collect but it didn't turn up. That's the only reason I had to drive out here.' She gives Von a smile and chuckles to herself. 'But I guess I collected more than I bargained for.'

He stares out the window at the flat, desolate landscape. A few tortured trees bend low to the ground, their trunks deformed by the forceful winds that blow here.

Ahinata clears her throat. 'Those trees are akeakes.'

The woman must be psychic, the way she read his mind. But then, he quickly realises, she probably saw him staring.

Now she points to her left. 'That's Te Whanga Lagoon.'

He sees a vast gold-tinged mirror that flows into the horizon. A scimitar-billed wading bird stabs the glass-like surface, sending circles of ripply waves dancing across the water.

'So,' asks Ahinata, 'what brought you to the islands?'

She's caught him off guard. He's not sure how to answer.

'My mother,' he says, eventually. 'I think she's bought a home here.'

'She's an islander, then?'

'Mum's an Aussie by birth but then she moved to Wellington. Her boyfriend Pete used to deck here on the islands. Mum told me she likes the Chathams — she sometimes came here with him.'

'What's her name?'

'Charlene,' he says. 'Charlene Taiaroa.'

Ahinata seems surprised. 'When I was a child, we had Taiaroas on the islands — that's an unusual name for an Aussie.'

'My dad's Moriori-Maori but they separated years ago. They never got a divorce — Mum still uses Taiaroa.'

The Torturer's fast asleep, sprawled across Von's lap. She's totally worn out with all the upheaval. It was kind of Ahinata to help them at the airport. But her questioning gets him down. She doesn't even know them. He was worried for a while, that she might be a spy from Welfare. But that's a stupid bloody thought. Not a soul, except for Henry, has the slightest clue they're over here.

Twenty minutes later they're at the Roos Roost. Ahinata stays with Stella while Von checks in at reception.

'I'm Sue,' a woman greets him. 'I've been waiting for you to get here. Your beds are all made up and there's a TV in the lounge room.' After taking his key, Von goes to fetch his sister.

The room's pretty basic with a pair of double bunks. But it's clean and bright; he's sure they'll be okay here. He tucks Stella into bed as Ahinata brings his backpack.

'I'll leave you to settle in but I'm sure you must be starving.

I'm popping in to see my daughter — shouldn't be more than an hour. After that I could take you home and cook you both some dinner. I live near Okawa which is a fair way up north. But there's plenty of room if you want to sleep over.'

The idea of dinner is more than tempting. They've only just arrived and he's got nothing here to feed them. Ahinata probably knows the islands; she could help him find their mother. But he doesn't know this person and he's worried about imposing. Ahinata's pretty cluey; she can sense Von's hesitation.

'It's okay,' she reassures him. 'And, I promise, I'm quite harmless. My daughter's due to have a baby — she lives here in Waitangi. We'll come back to town first thing in the morning. I'm going to help her paint the nursery.'

'Thanks,' he says. 'I do feel pretty hungry. If you can drive us back in the morning, it'd be great to have some dinner.'

The air is turning cold. Von adjusts his sister's doona. A strong wind's blown up; now it's hammering at the window. As he stares at the looming cloudbank, he thinks about his mother. He still can't believe that she's actually bought a home here.

He unpacks his kit, gives himself an insulin shot. Stella's medicine's nearly due but he'll leave it till after dinner. It makes her feel sick when she's got an empty tummy. He glances at his watch — Ahinata should be back soon. He pulls on a warmer jumper then gently wakes his sister.

Detective Tapper scowls as he flips through Von's diary. Jack's been trying to explain himself at Wellington City Headquarters.

'Von called me when she didn't come home. As I said before, that was a couple of days ago.' They're covering old ground, the whole process is frustrating. He told the detective this when he first phoned from Fremantle. Jack's still not sure whether to mention Charlene's beating — he's afraid it may imply she's involved with her boyfriend's business. The fact that Von's searching for her now suggests he may know where to find her. Jack's reluctant to cause unnecessary trouble.

'I know Charlene — it's not the first time she's done this. When we were together she often disappeared for weeks.'

'Weeks?'

Jack eyeballs Tapper. His approach is getting them nowhere. 'Yes, she'd go on these benders — I told you, she had a problem with amphetamines.'

The detective stops and puts down his pen. 'I'm sorry Jack; we've gone over this before. It's just the timing of things, we need to be certain. A woman's disappeared and now, it would appear, both her kids are missing. She worked at Endorphin

— a nightclub down on Vivian Street. This morning we received a disturbing report. Another dancer, Kristie Nichol, has gone missing from the club. We've reason to believe she's a close friend of Charlene's.'

Tapper pauses. He stares at Jack intently. 'Two women have disappeared, the circumstances are suspicious. Things aren't looking good; we could be dealing with foul play, Jack.'

The gravity of the news slowly penetrates Jack's senses. He breaks into a sweat, feels overcome with nausea.

Tapper gives him a moment before he continues.

'We can assume from Von's diary that he's searching for his mother. As you already know, Ms Watts saw the kids yesterday — a sixteen year old and a toddler, it's unlikely they'd go far. But you know your son best. Have you any thoughts on where he could be looking?'

Jack's mind is alive with horrifying images.

'I've no idea,' he says at last. 'Von doesn't know Wellington. And we only spoke briefly when he called about his mother.' Jack realises now, he's going to have to tell him. 'She was assaulted, you know, by an associate of her partner — a dealer as far as I know.'

The detective's face hardens. 'Pete Mullins,' he snaps, 'we've been looking for her boyfriend. Why didn't you mention this before?'

'I'm sorry,' Jack says. 'Von didn't want me involved; I wasn't sure how much to tell you.'

Tapper shakes his head in frustration. 'It's our job to find your wife; the smallest detail can help us. When Von mentioned the dealer did he give you a description?'

'No,' Jack replies, wishing he could help more. 'His info

was pretty sketchy — something about the police and this dealer chasing Pete.'

'At least it's a start. Are you sure you've told me everything?'

Jack gives him a nod. He's had enough of talking.

'Why don't we leave it for now but if you think of anything else, call me on this number.'

Jack pockets the detective's card; picks up his luggage.

'Thought I'd be staying with the boy; I'll need to find accommodation. But here's my mobile number — don't hesitate to call me.'

Von and Stella have vanished; Charlene may have come to grief. Jack wears a cloak of despair as he walks the streets of Wellington. He should be looking for a room but instead he's out here wandering. He lets his heart lead the way as he's drawn towards the harbour. The smells, the sounds of the ocean — they're Jack's link to something deeper. He digs into his pocket, pulls out Charlene's sketch. She must have sensed something in Von; something buried in his nature. The boy's always had a struggle connecting with their culture. Jack's done his best to guide him but it's driven a wedge between them. But Charlene saw him as Moriori; could she feel his bond with Rekohu? As Jack puts down his bag, he feels himself shiver. The expression on Von's face, it's proud, almost arrogant. It reminds him of Koche, one of their brave, rebellious ancestors. Koche never gave up — he kept escaping his enslavers. Now Von's run away, a fugitive from Welfare. Drifting deeper into the drawing, Jack listens to his instincts: his heart opens up — the ancestors are calling. They reached him once before, let him know his dad was dying. As a picture slowly forms in his mind, Jack knows where Von will be. He even gave the boy his fare before he left for Wellington.

Enveloped in darkness, the Cockroach punches through the bush. Lit up by the old car's headlights, a track of battered limestone winds its way towards a cottage. When the home appears, it's small and made of weatherboard. The makeshift fence, Von is told, was constructed out of whale bone.

They move inside. Ahinata makes them comfortable. She fires up the heater and switches on the TV.

Half an hour later, they're all sitting around the table. With a texture that reminds Von of crayfish, the dish is laced with heaven. Even Stella, who won't touch fish, is hoeing straight in.

'What is this?' he asks. 'The flavour's totally awesome.'

Ahinata laughs. 'Chatham Island blue cod, we catch it all the time here.' She piles up their plates with more fish and salad. 'Your ancestors ate this cod — they used to catch it off the rock shelves.' Now her eyes draw Von in. She's searching for something. 'I'm sure you would know — they were peace-loving people. We're the same, you and I; my blood is Moriori.'

Von's blown away by this sudden revelation. Apart from his dad, he's never met another Moriori.

'That's incredible,' he says. 'My dad would love to meet

you. He's always talking about that stuff. He says there aren't too many of us left now.'

'There're quite a few on the Chathams; even more on the mainland. I've lived here all my life. But when I was a kid, I knew nothing about our history. There was an unwritten rule; no-one ever spoke of it.'

'Yeah, Dad told me how his father mostly hid that he was Moriori. My gran's Ngati Mutunga — she hated talking about the past. Dad thinks she was embarrassed because her tribe was one of the invaders.'

Ahinata looks upset as she nods her agreement. 'The Taranaki invasion. When the two Maori tribes arrived to claim new territory, hundreds of Moriori were savagely killed and eaten. Our heads were thrown to their hounds — we were chewed on like dog food. But our ancestors — karapuna — kept their covenant of peace; even faced with all that loss, they wouldn't fight the invaders. No-one tried to help them — not the European settlers or the crews from visiting ships. Maybe they were trying to protect their own safety. The atrocities and enslavement continued for decades. If your blood was Moriori, a dog was treated better.'

A silence falls between them. They've torn the past wide open. Von knows it all but it's never had such impact before. Maybe it's being here on Rekohu — the ancestors seem much closer.

'Ahinata,' he asks, carefully. 'Do you ever feel confused?'

'In what way, son?'

'Well, Dad's raised me as a Moriori. He's always tried to make me proud of that. But there's also Ngati Mutunga blood flowing in my veins.'

'Many of us trace back to the Taranaki invaders. One of my own ancestors was a Ngati Mutunga warrior. It's inevitable, when you think about it.'

'It's just occasionally I wonder, where do I fit in?'

'What does your heart tell you?'

Von's thoughts drift off to another time on Rekohu; a peaceful time, a spiritual time, a time when people lived their lives in harmony with nature. But soon his mind fills up with images of slaughter. There's a shadow on his heart when he thinks about what followed. 'Our people lived in peace for centuries. They didn't deserve that terror.'

'I couldn't agree more. And I think you have your answer.'

When dinner's finished they settle in the lounge room. Stella's in front of the fire, happily devouring a huge bowl of ice-cream. Bees chase Winnie the Pooh across a state-of-the-art widescreen.

'Your sister's a good wee thing. Most kids get clingy when their mum's not around.'

'We haven't been seeing that much of her. Mum has to work nights — during the day she tries to sleep.'

Ahinata looks concerned. She sits down next to Stella. 'You said your mother's bought a home here. Isn't it a bit strange that she didn't come to meet you?'

Von feels embarrassed. How does he explain their situation? 'Mum's been missing for days; I'm not sure we're going to find her. This heavy dealer guy's been after her and I think she might be hiding.' He pulls out the receipt, quickly hands it over. 'After I found this I thought she might be over here. But really, when you think about it, anything could have happened.'

Ahinata frowns as she studies the receipt. 'Kaingaroa's not that far. Why don't we take a look on our way back to Waitangi? And I'll give John Clarke a call — he's our local cop on Rekohu. He's usually the first to know when someone new arrives here.'

'No,' Von blurts out. He didn't mean to sound so panicky. If the police get involved he's certain they'll take Stella.

'But he's probably your best chance of finding your mother.'

Von's stomach tightens when he imagines what could happen. They'll split them apart — put his sister in an orphanage. But Ahinata puts two and two together.

'What is it, son? Are you running from something?'

Running back into town, Jack heads for a travel shop. There's one in the mall not far from Charlene's place in Cuba Street. Wellington's shutting down but luckily the store's still open. After pushing through the door, he's approached by an assistant.

'Good evening,' he says, to the pretty young woman. 'Any chance I could book a flight to the Chathams?'

'We're about to close,' Keira says, 'but I'll see what I can do.' When she takes Jack's name, she's surprised by the coincidence. 'That's interesting,' she says, as she gives him a look. 'I sent another Mr Taiaroa to the Chathams just this morning.'

'Really,' Jack says calmly, though his heart's already racing. 'It's a fairly common name; wouldn't go reading too much into it.' He can't believe his luck; wants to ask straight out what this Mr Taiaroa looked like. But he knows from experience: he'll learn more if he's patient.

The girl checks him out with her striking hazel eyes. She's wearing half a smile. Jack's feeling a bit uncomfortable.

'What?' he asks. It comes out far too rudely.

'I'm sorry,' Keira says. 'But you're freaking me out here. The other Mr Taiaroa was travelling with his sister. He was much younger and slighter; it's just your faces look so similar.'

Jack leans back in his chair — he can't stop smiling. 'I knew it,' he says. 'I bloody well knew it.'

Later that evening Jack finds himself a room. The wait is frustrating but there's nothing he can do. His flight doesn't leave till the day after tomorrow. Young Keira was very helpful, organised all his accommodation. She booked two rooms at Chatham Lodge, that way the kids can stay there with him.

He's read about the lodge. In fact, he's always dreamed of visiting. It overlooks Lake Marakapia on his ancestral land at Henga. There's a grove of kopi trees that leads down to the sea and Moriori middens are dotted through the sand dunes. Jack wishes their stay was under different circumstances. They could have wandered amongst the kopis, following the footprints of karapuna. But this time around that definitely won't be possible.

He keeps imagining his son trying to be a father. Von's got a good heart and he's very kind to animals. But two-year-old kids are a totally different matter. Jack knows only too well, he's going to have his hands full. Now he's wondering what to say when they finally catch up. What can he possibly do to minimise the damage? Charlene's disappeared, foul play is suspected. Hopefully Von has information that could help the investigation. As Jack prays to his ancestors for their wisdom and guidance, he clings to the hope that the police have got it wrong. Nothing's certain yet; she could still be on a bender.

Jack thinks about calling Tapper but something makes him stop. Von's obviously avoiding Welfare but what if there's more to it. He had his fare to the Chathams, but Jack was certain he'd never use it. And down at Wellington Harbour, when the ancestors touched his heart — they painted him a picture, Jack could see his son on Rekohu. Was Von feeling the same pull? Have karapuna reached him? He wrote in his diary that he had to find his mother. And he told Jack himself, Charlene's been to the islands.

Jack concedes that he's probably grasping at straws. Has Von flown to the Chathams because he thinks his mother's over there? Instead of ringing Tapper, Jack tries the Roos Roost. But the phone rings forever and nobody answers.

He breathes in the salty air at Kaingaroa Harbour. A crescent of white sand hems the jagged coastline. Waves break onto the shore, their crests tinged with foam and aqua. A few metres off the beach, rocks rise like tall black sentries. They're protecting something sacred — there's definitely a presence here. Stella's squawking like a seagull as she gathers up bright shells. Ahinata shows her a feather before joining Von at the shoreline.

'Can you hear them?' she asks. 'They're all through the islands.'

He knows this tranquil place has seen its share of sorrow. He closes his eyes; tries to work out what he's feeling.

'I'm not sure,' he says. 'I'm picking up some sadness.'

'You feel their spirits,' she says, 'the spirits of karapuna. Tamakororo, one of the ancestors, was killed on this beach. Skirmish Bay, that's what the Englishmen called it.'

Ahinata stares out to sea. She's gone very quiet. Von leaves her with her thoughts and goes to fetch the Torturer. Both her shoes have been ditched; her pants are getting wet. She wants to swim but the water's bloody freezing.

'Let's go,' he says, trying to distract her. 'Mama's house is up there. Are you going to help me find her?'

They race through the shallows back to Ahinata. 'Can we leave now?' he urges. 'That woman from Welfare might show up — we really need to find our mother.'

'Yes, of course,' she says. But there's a moment's hesitation. Ahinata's mouth says one thing — her eyes reveal another. Uncertain why, Von's pretty sure she's stalling.

Passing Kaingaroa Club, they head down a street that sweeps around the harbour. The road's a work of art. Chips of jewel-like paua shell glisten in the sun. Stella tries to pick one up but it's glued into the surface. Perched behind the harbour there's a clutch of beach-style cottages. Ahinata points out a shanty with a caravan attachment.

'Are you sure?' Von asks.

She nods her confirmation.

It's not the sort of home he'd imagine Charlene buying. An old Harley Fat Boy is crouching in the drive. Wet towels hang on the line; the front door's slightly open.

'All right,' he says, excited. 'Let's find out if she's in there!'

But once again, Ahinata dawdles.

'What is it?' he asks. 'Is there something you're not telling me?'

'This house has been on the market for quite a while. And I know, for a fact, it's still occupied by squatters.'

'But if someone bought the place, they'd have to move out, right?'

'Squatting laws are complicated. It's not quite that simple. I'm just trying to warn you; a total stranger probably lives here.'

Ahinata means well but she's not making sense If Charlene's bought this place then it's hers; end of story. And if anyone wants to argue, he's got the receipt to prove it. After hammering on the door, he can't help feeling anxious. If Charlene is inside, what's he supposed to say to her? *Oh, hi there Mum, we're the kids you must have forgotten.* Soon a huge bikie guy is looming in the doorway. Von's pretty tall but this bloke's even bigger. He looks a bit stoned — either that or he's been napping.

'G'day,' Von says nervously. 'Is Charlene Taiarca home?'

The bikie looks dumbfounded. He stares at Von sourly. 'Charlene?' he mumbles. 'Mate, I've never even heard of her.'

'Is Pete here then? He sometimes calls himself the Seagull?'

'No,' the guy snaps. 'I'm the only person living here.'

Von takes a deep breath. He pulls out the receipt, starts flapping it at the bikie. 'See this,' he says. 'My mother's bought this property.'

After snatching the receipt, the bikie screws it into a ball and drops it on the doorstep. 'I don't know this Charlene chick so you'd better piss off out of here.'

'Don't bullshit me, man. I know my mother's in there.'

The door slams shut. Von's left standing on the doorstep. After salvaging the receipt, Ahinata drags him back. Then she steps up to the door and starts banging away impatiently. When the bikie guy returns, he's not impressed to see her.

'Get lost,' he barks. 'You're trespassing on private property.'

Ahinata glares; she's not taking a backward step. 'Young man,' she scolds, 'you've got disgusting manners.' He's twice her size. Von's astonished by her courage. He watches in awe as she reads the giant the Riot Act.

Great, he thinks, as they drive back to Waitangi — the bikie's lived there for over four years; didn't even know the house was on the market.

'I'm sorry, son. I can see you're disappointed.'

Disappointed? More like full-on bloody panicked. He turns around and stares at little Stella. What in god's name possessed him to bring her here? And if Charlene's not on Rekohu, where on the planet is she?

'Von, I'm not convinced that squatter was being truthful. Word travels fast here on the Chathams. The place was up for sale — I'm certain he must know that. But there's something else, I'm not sure if you've realised.'

'What?' he asks, hoping for good news.

'The receipt for your mother's house — well, it was only for the deposit. There's nothing to say that the sale was ever settled.'

Von's surprised he didn't think of that. 'I'd better find out but I'm not sure how.'

Ahinata gives him a wink. 'One of my friends works at the bank; she discharges all the mortgages. If the sale's gone through, she should know a few of the details.'

Ahinata needs to see her daughter but she arranges to meet Von later. It's just before ten when she drops him at the backpackers'.

'Follow the road that leads down to the sea. You can't miss Waitangi pub — I'll see you there around eleven. We'll have a chat with some of the locals; they might have news about your mother.'

There's more than an hour to kill — Von takes Stella back to their room. He dumps his gear on the carpet, collapses onto the bunk bed. He feels numb — no, depressed. Nothing's turned out how he hoped here. It was totally insane dragging Stella to these islands — for all he knows, Charlene could be safely home now. He gets a sudden urge to go and call his mother, but he's worried Welfare could trace him from her phone line. In the end he decides against it. Henry would have been in touch if she'd turned up at the apartment. Stella's looking bored; she stares blankly out the window. But the pub's right near the beach. They might as well head down there.

Stella scurries onto the sand like a crazy little crab. She's a trapped thing set free as she dances near the water. Von pulls off his runners, feels the grit beneath his feet. But soon a dreadful sense of sadness begins to overcome him. He hears weeping in the wind — the death cries of his people. His eyes drift around the coastline; there's a chain of butchered bodies. Sorrow drifts up through the sand, touching the deepest part of him. The stain of spilt blood lies just beneath the surface.

He feels tugging on his jeans; Stella's wrapped herself around him.

'Vonny's sad,' she cries. She's giving him a cuddle. He picks her up, tries to reassure her. But this sorrow that he feels has completely overwhelmed him. Jack's told him that people still find bones on Rekohu. A few years ago a woman's skeleton was found, her arms wrapped in an embrace around the bones of her small baby. Here, on this beach, Von can feel the pain and death. Stella clings to him, fiercely; she needs someone to hold on to.

'Don't cry,' he says, cradling her tiny body. 'You don't have to be scared — we're going to find your mama.'

Soon they're sitting around a table in the Hotel Waitangi. But his mind's still on the beach, reliving what occurred there. He feels the same sense of loss when he thinks about his mother. Ahinata calls to a waiter to bring some drinks and tucker.

'You're quiet,' she says. 'Is everything okay?'

How can he describe it? This experience is all new to him. Today, on that beach, something seriously deep went down. The ancestors touched his soul — now he knows they're really out there.

'I felt karapuna on the beach. They were showing me their terror.'

'You're not the first,' she replies. 'I've seen that look before. When the rains are soft and the mists are lying low, I swear it feels like the whole island's weeping.'

A pot of tea arrives and a soft drink for Stella. Ahinata pours Von a cup, stirring in a couple of sugars.

'Drink up,' she urges. 'Sweet tea calms the nerves.'

'Not mine,' he explains. 'I'm a bloody diabetic.'

Ahinata laughs. He's glad she sees the funny side. She pours another cup then leans across the table.

'I've just spoken with some locals — there's no word about your mother. But I rang my friend who works at the bank in Waitangi. She said the Kaingaroa sale has definitely been settled. She remembers discharging the mortgage from the previous owner. I'm sorry, Von, that's all she could tell me. No names or details — she can't breach customer confidentiality.'

A tiny seed of hope starts growing inside him. The sale's gone through; Charlene might be over here. Ahinata passes Von a sandwich as she slowly sips her cuppa.

'Apparently a lawyer on the mainland acted for the vendor — I've got his details.'

'Vendor?' Von asks, confused.

'The owner,' she explains, 'the person who sold the house. The lawyer's your best bet — he'll know who bought the property. Son, my daughter's waiting; it's time I helped her with the nursery. But if you like, I can give him a call later.'

Von could phone himself but he doesn't feel that confident. He's never spoken to a lawyer — he'd prefer to let her deal with it. 'Thanks,' he says, though it seems a bit inadequate. 'You've been really great but you hardly even know me.'

Ahinata studies him again with those sharp, inquiring eyes. 'But I do,' she says, 'and karapuna know you too. You're not alone on this journey. There's a reason why you came here.'

Her words make him shiver. He wonders what she's saying. Since Charlene left when he was six, Von's always felt alone. Sure, his dad was around, but things were just so different. A huge hole of sadness somehow forced its way between them. Stella's only two; she shouldn't have to feel that pain. That's the reason he's here. She can't grow up without her mother.

Ahinata stands up to leave. She tells Von not to worry. 'Hopefully by tomorrow we'll have a bit more news. In the morning, if you're interested, I'll pick you both up early. There's a Moriori grove that I'd really like to show you.'

Chucking his mobile on the dresser, Jack collapses into a chair. He's just taken a call from Tapper about an overdose at the harbour. Kristie Nichol was found dead, her body pumped full of amphetamines. The forensics team have finished and they're certain it was homicide. Jack's still trying to come to terms with what the detective told him — Charlene's disappearance has been upgraded to a possible murder case. He feels incredibly sad for Kristie Nichol's family. It's not hard to imagine the hurt they must be feeling. Losing one of your kids that way would have to be unbearable — only twenty-two, her journey was just beginning. His knuckles glow white as he clenches his fists; Tapper needs to know that Von is on the islands. But whenever he tries to tell him, Jack feels like he's being gagged. His heart's guided by karapuna and he knows he's got to trust them. All this waiting around frustrates him; he's itching to be on Rekohu. Those kids will need support if it's bad news for their mother. He keeps trying to reach Von but there's trouble with his mobile. And the phone just rings out whenever he calls the backpackers'.

Now he gazes out the window at the beautiful hills of Wellington. With all this time to kill he should go and see his mother. He often visualises Mary and the chasm that's grown between them. Is that trench too deep — would she want to see him? Not a word has passed between them since they argued at the funeral. In the days before Riwai's death, the old man heard his ancestors calling. He even asked if his body could be laid to rest on Rekohu. But Mary refused to take him home — she said they'd made their life in Wellington. Jack still wonders, to this day, why she wouldn't listen. Was it grief or maybe shame? What drove her final decision? Riwai's heart belonged to Rekohu. He wanted to be buried there.

Just a few hours later in Oriental Bay, Jack's sitting in a hire car outside the family villa. It's a beautiful old home, the one his parents worked so hard for. In Jack's imagination, he's a young child again. He remembers scaling his favourite tree; spraining his skinny leg when he swung off the balcony. The little boy inside him wants to charge up those steps, rush through the door and let his mother hug him. He sees movement at one of the windows — knows she must be in there. Slowly, he turns away, puts the key in the ignition. Not yet, he tells himself, maybe one day I'll be ready. He owes it to Riwai to take him home to Rekohu. But Mary's fighting her own demons and he has to find a way to help her.

As Jack turns the key, his thoughts return to his boy. Ever since Von left for Wellington his journey's been fraught with danger. When Charlene reached out to him, Von could easily have slammed the door on her. But he gave his mum a chance. Jack sees a lesson for himself there.

Surrounded by kopi in a grove at Hapupu, Von's skin breaks out in goose bumps — he knows he's not alone here. The climate in the grove is peaceful but unsettling. Beyond lichen-covered trees a strong wind howls, but here, in nature's sanctuary, sound has been suspended. A mist of soft rain drifts down through the canopy. Ancient spirits fill the air; karapuna are all around him. A laughing heart-shaped face stares out from one of the kopis — a snap-shot tapped in bark, created by their fingers. *He sees them gathered together planting a kopi — perhaps to celebrate the birth of a baby — hears them chanting to their gods as they praise the power of nature.*

His thoughts turn to Charlene. Could she possibly have been here? She's his mother, she gave birth to him — did karapuna touch her too? Her face forms in his mind but she fades away too quickly. Now he prays to his ancestors — asks them to protect her.

Stella squats at the base of a kopi, staring at a carving. Ahinata smiles at Von; her eyes look deep and thoughtful.

'How was it?' she asks.

'Incredible,' he says. 'You can feel them all around you.' It's impossible to explain the depth of his experience.

'I know what you mean — this place affects us all. And depending on the day, you feel different types of energy. Sometimes when I come here I'm overwhelmed with grief. Seeing the carvings, their ancient faces; it fills me with such sadness. But the next time I visit, I'll feel a sense of continuity — those images have survived for hundreds of years. That gives me real hope for the future of our people.'

A fierce wind blows up when they reach the edge of the grove. Ahinata stops and gently taps a kopi.

'If we're going to catch some flounder we'll need a little help. Karapuna had magic rites; their ways were very tapu. If they needed help with fishing, they always tapped a kopi.'

They climb back into the Cockroach and Ahinata does a U-turn.

'Thought we'd drive to Blind Jim's; it's on the shore of the lagoon. I've packed a picnic lunch but we'll need some fish for dinner.'

His mind drifts off as he stares out the window. Charlene's constantly in his thoughts, he desperately needs to find her. But standing amongst the kopis, he'd felt himself relax — a blanket of calm somehow wrapped itself around him.

Stella's first out of the car when they reach the lagoon. A spray of sand marks her course as she runs along the shoreline. She seems happy enough now but Von knows what she's been going through. She cries herself to sleep; keeps shouting for her mama. He's relieved to see her laugh again — it was a good idea to come here. Ahinata gives him a smile. She's tuned-in to what he's thinking. When she tried to reach the lawyer, the office was unattended. But she left an urgent message and she's hoping for good news later.

Out on the lagoon, there's an extraordinary array of bird-life.

'Didn't know you had black swans here.'

'They build their nests around the edge of the lagoon — the European settlers really loved their swan eggs. Even today, the islanders enjoy them.'

The idea of eating swan eggs doesn't sit well with Von. He's used to black swans being fiercely protected — they're the much loved emblem of Western Australia.

Ahinata squats down, starts fossicking through some sea shells. 'We find shark's teeth here — so old they're actually fossilised.'

Von fumbles through his pockets, retrieving Charlene's present. 'Mum found this here when she visited the Chathams.' As he stares at the fossil, he feels acutely lonely.

Soon they're camped on a tartan rug, soaking up the sunshine, as they fill their hungry faces with crusty bread and crayfish. A plane buzzes across the sky, invading the peaceful warmth. Ahinata stands up, lifts her arms and stretches.

'It's a perfect day for fishing. Why don't we spear ourselves some flounder?'

Jack drags his suitcase into the tiny airport terminal and finds Stan, from the lodge, waiting there to meet him. As they head towards a tour bus that's sitting out the front, Stan learns why his guest is visiting the Chathams. Jack's amused to discover he's the one and only passenger. After climbing into the driver's seat, Stan swiftly starts the engine.

'The kids are at the Roos Roost.' Jack's anxious to see Von. 'Could we pick them up and bring them back for dinner?'

Stan gives him a nod. 'Of course, we'll head straight over.'

It's Jack's first time on Rekohu. For so long he's dreamt of being here. But as he gazes out the window he sees nothing of the lagoon. He stares vacantly into space, his mind lost in worries.

'I won't be long,' he tells Stan when they reach the Roos Roost. 'Just need to settle the bill and help them pack their stuff up.'

While Jack's wandering around the building looking for the entrance, a tall, friendly woman hurries out to help him.

After quickly introducing himself, he explains his situation.

'But the kids aren't here. They've gone out with Ahinata.'

'Ahinata?'

'That's right. She picked them up early.'

Jack can't hide his alarm. 'Who on earth is Ahinata?' Von doesn't know a soul here on the Chathams.

Sue tries to talk calmly. 'Don't worry,' she says. 'She's a very close friend of mine. When the kids showed up alone she took them under her wing. She was only trying to help — they were in a spot of trouble.'

Jack's thoughts are in turmoil. He should have got here sooner. 'I've phoned this place so many times. It's bloody frustrating, no-one ever answers. And it's the same with my son; I can't reach him on his mobile.'

Sue looks embarrassed. 'Our phone's out of order, I'm really sorry about that. And you can't use cell phones here on the Chathams. But your kids should be back soon — they've been out since early this morning.'

His patience has gone. He can't wait any longer. 'Have you any idea where I might find them?'

'Ahinata's giving Von a tour of some Moriori sites.'

'Anywhere round here I can hire a car?'

'No need,' says Sue. 'Old Stan will drive you out there.'

Standing at Manukau Point, stung by wind and spray, Von stares into the void of a lonely grey seascape. His ancestors didn't journey into these seas, but if they had, they most certainly would have perished. Ten thousand kilometres of endless, icy ocean stretches between Manukau and the southern coast of Chile. Manukau, he's been told, means place of many birds. Now a huge flock of gulls is circling above him. On a nearby hill there's an old family graveyard. Tommy Solomon lies there; the last full-blood Moriori. Two pilot whale skulls guard the entrance to his statue.

Taking Stella's hand, Ahinata leads them to the rock shelf.

'Manukau was once a Moriori village. There was a seal colony close by and when the tide was low, people gathered seafood from these rocks. Things like paua and crayfish, urchins and limpets. They caught delicious blue cod off this very platform. And blackfish — that's pilot whales — sometimes stranded up the coast. The ancestors believed they were gifts from the sea gods.'

'Dad said whales are linked with human death.'

'That's right,' she confirms. 'When a Moriori died, a stranding often followed.'

After pointing out some paua beneath the shallow water, she starts levering off huge shells and filling up her bucket. 'If you mince the flesh up finely, they make delicious patties.' They speared half-a-dozen flounder back at Te Whanga: looks like paua and fish on the menu for dinner.

Ahinata seems surprised, there's a tour bus pulling up. 'Stan's out here late. It's not the usual time for tourists.'

Soon her bucket's full and they stroll back towards the statue. Standing beside Tommy is a tall, dark figure. If he didn't know better, Von would swear it was his dad. But the closer he gets, the more undeniable it becomes. Flanking the giant statue is Jack, his own father. If one wasn't made of stone, the two figures could be brothers.

Rushing straight over, Jack crushes Von in his hug. 'Thank God, son, you're all right — I've been worried out of my brain.' Squeezing Von's cheeks, Jack's eyes fill up with moisture. 'Thank God,' he says again. 'I'm so relieved to see you.'

Von's too stunned to respond. How on earth did Jack find him?

Ahinata moves away and tries to take Stella with her. But the Torturer won't go. She puts her arms up to be cuddled.

'What are you doing here?' Von asks. He's secretly glad to see his father.

'I'd like to ask you the same thing. I fly to Wellington and there's not a bloody trace of you. You needed help,' Jack adds flatly. 'I couldn't hang around in Freo.'

'We've had a few problems — that's why I had to leave the

apartment. A Welfare woman was after Stella and this probably sounds insane, but I think Mum's bought a house here.'

Jack looks surprised. 'A house, here on Rekohu?'

'It's weird, I know. But remember what I told you — she's spent time on the Chathams.' Pulling the receipt from his pocket, Von quickly hands it over.

'Kaingaroa,' Jack mumbles as he studies the piece of paper.

'That's right. But a bikie squatter's living there.'

Jack shakes his head in confusion. Ahinata comes to join them.

'Kia ora!' she says, brightly. 'You must be Von's father.' Jack takes her hand, kisses both her cheeks. They chat politely for a moment and then he turns to the Torturer.

'And you must be Stella?' His hands reach out to her. But Stella withdraws in a panic; starts scrambling up Von's trousers. Jack turns to Ahinata and whispers a few words. After giving him the nod, she puts Stella on one hip and heads towards the tour bus.

Von and his father walk along in silence. They find refuge on a rock that overlooks the ocean. When Jack begins to talk he sounds a thousand miles away.

'Don't know if I ever told you, but your mother was eighteen when she captured me in the savannah.'

'You met Mum in Africa?'

Jack lets out a laugh, but it's thin and lacking humour. 'I'd moved to Perth from Wellington, didn't know a soul in Western Australia. It was a sunny Saturday morning and I'd read that the zoo had an African savannah. Thought I'd go and check out the big cats. Charlene had the same idea, she was touring with a dance troupe — all these bright young sparks fresh out of Sydney. I saw this pint-sized princess in baggy denim overalls. *Come and I'll show you my amazing brown boobies*' — those were the very first words your mother ever spoke to me. She hit without warning — just bowled up out of nowhere.'

Von's heard about animal magnetism but this sounds really crazy. 'She must have been insane. The second you met, she wants to flash her boobs at you!'

'It was strange,' Jack agrees with a wry little smile. 'And she was mad, all right, in the best possible way. But as usual, mate, you haven't been listening. She said boobies, not boobs — I haven't finished my story yet.'

Acutely aware that his gut is turning over, Von wonders why his father's bringing up ancient history. The wind could freeze your nuts off but Jack's sweating all over. Now he's wiping at his face with a red-chequered hanky. Von searches his father's eyes but all he finds is sorrow. Is it because he bolted from Wellington? All this sentimental talk could be leading to a lecture. But the pain in Jack's face says there's more going on. He's never been good at hiding his feelings.

'What is it?' Von asks. 'There's something you want to tell me.'

'Charlene loved birds; that's what she was trying to show me.' Jack's crying now. Von doesn't know how to help him. 'She wanted me to see her beautiful brown boobies. I've never seen anyone so excited, and all because of these big brown seagulls.'

'Her boyfriend's called the Seagull.'

Jack doesn't seem to hear him. 'Son,' he says. Now he's fumbling with Von's hand. 'When I arrived in Wellington the authorities were at the apartment. There's no easy way to tell you. God knows, I've just been trying.'

Welfare Jenny, Von thinks, trying to get her paws on Stella. 'It's okay,' he tells his dad. 'They're not going to take my sister.'

Jack's expression hasn't changed. He stares at Von grimly.

'I've been talking with a detective down at police headquarters.' He pauses for a moment, grips Von's hand harder. 'I really hate to tell you this, son. It's not good news. There's a chance your mum's been murdered.'

Jack reaches out but Von pushes him away. His father's talking shit. No-one's killed his mother. He turns to the tour bus when he hears his sister crying.

'Stella's scared,' he tells Jack. 'She really needs me.'

Von rushes towards the bus. Stella meets him halfway. When he scoops her up, her tiny body feels like jelly.

Ahinata looks upset. 'I couldn't comfort her,' she explains. 'She was trying to be brave but she's had too much to deal with.'

Von shoots his dad a look as he holds his baby sister. His mother can't be dead; he's only just got to know her. And if it's true, what does that mean for Stella?

'What's Stella supposed to do? She can't survive without her mother.'

'Son,' Jack says, softly, 'I know this is a shock. But watch what you say in front of the little one.'

Stella's crying subsides as she clings onto Von. He'd like to find a nice safe cave and hide in there forever.

'We're a team, me and Stella — Mum wasn't around much anyway. All those years she was gone, I managed fine without her. And this kid, she's tough — I doubt she'll even miss her.'

Now he can't stop the tears. Von knows his words were nasty. *Don't let her be dead,* he prays. *Charlene's special. She's my mother.*

Guiding his son back to Stan's bus, Jack desperately wants to help; the boy's turning completely in on himself. Stella's eyes look weary. She's still draped across Von's shoulder. Sliding into a seat, he gently cradles her on his lap Jack has to swallow hard, seeing his son so tender. He can sense how close they are. They've clearly been through a lot together. A part of him feels awful for breaking such horrible news, but at least it came from him — not some stranger in a uniform.

Stan's driving cross-country, Ahinata's bumping along behind. The bus tosses them around as they head for Chatham Lodge. When Stan turns left up a long limestone drive, Jack can see Lake Marakapia spreading out before him. He's never seen the place before but there's an ache of recognition. Riwai grew up near this lake — it touches something lost inside him. He turns to his son; tries to find the words to tell him. 'This is Henga,' he says softly, 'your ancestral homeland. I'm just sorry we're not here in happier circumstances.'

Von nods at his father and turns towards the lake. But Jack regrets bringing it up. His timing's bloody terrible. The boy's only thoughts will be fears about his mother.

A woman's waiting on the verandah as they climb down off the bus. Her eyes are kind but shy when she walks across to meet them.

'You must be Jack,' she says, relinquishing a smile. 'I'm Jean, Stan's wife. Welcome to Chatham Lodge.'

'This is my son Von and his little half-sister.'

Jean reacts with concern when there's no response from Stella. 'This child's exhausted,' she announces, 'and I don't like her colour. Helen, one of my staff, is a registered nurse. I'll make sure she has a look at her.'

Ahinata wanders up with her catch of fish and paua. There's an ease between the women. Jack can see they've got a history.

'What's this?' Jean laughs, as she takes the heavy bucket.

'Just my small contribution — you weren't expecting me for dinner.'

Stella starts to cough and Jean shepherds them all inside. After settling them in the lounge room, she switches on the TV.

'I'll get Helen, now,' she says. 'It's time we attended to this little one.'

'I'm sorry,' Von says, looking a bit alarmed. 'Stella's medicine's due but I left it in my bag. I didn't know we were coming here — all our stuff's at the Roos Roost.'

'Don't worry,' Stan says. 'I'll take a run over there while dinner's cooking.'

After Jean and Stan have left them, Jack turns to Ahinata.

'Listen,' he says. 'I appreciate everything you've done. You've been so good to these kids — I really want to thank you.'

Ahinata stands up, casually shrugs her shoulder. 'It's the least I could do; they're new to the Chathams. Now you need to be alone so I'm off to mince that paua.'

Jack clears his throat to get his son's attention. When Von won't respond he clumsily starts a conversation.

'Ahinata seems nice — she's been showing you around?'

Von takes his time to answer. 'Yeah,' he says eventually, 'she's part-Moriori. We've been checking out some sites — Hapupu was amazing.'

Jack lets out a sigh. At last Von's opening up. 'That's fascinating, son. I'd love to chat about it later.' Then he says, carefully, 'What I told you before, about the police and what they're thinking. Nothing's written in stone. They haven't found her body.'

'But you reckon they probably will?'

Jack's about to answer when Jean returns with Helen.

'We'll see Stella now. Helen wants to check her temperature.' While the two women fuss, Jack takes Von to the window.

'Over there,' he says. 'That's Lake Marakapia.'

Von turns to face his father. His eyes demand an answer. 'Come on, Dad,' he says, 'what about my question?'

It's not Jack's nature to be negative. He'd like to offer Von some hope. But he can't mislead the boy. There's not a lot of hope to cling to. 'The police in Wellington have grave concerns for your mum. She's not the only cancer to go missing from Endorphin. There was another, Kristie Nichol — her body was found two days ago.'

Von's face is drained of colour. 'Mum's friend was called Kristie; she worked at Endorphin. We never met but she used to help with Stella.'

'I'm so sorry; it's an awful bloody business. But the police are convinced the disappearances are linked. Not much more I can say. We just have to wait and see, son.'

Memories cling to Von's heart like a painful bloody stain. This silent wave of sadness is drowning every part of him. He keeps seeing Charlene's face, imagining the terror she must have gone through. But he can't accept that he'll never hear her voice again. He thinks about her life; all the bad shit that's happened — she seemed so afraid those days before she vanished. Even Henry tried to tell him, but he didn't want to listen. He was so caught up in his stupid Wild Mother Chase. That awful belting from Pete's partner — it's all crossed Von's mind before. Rob must have been the freak Henry spotted with poor Kristie. Charlene went missing first: what hope does that leave for his mother?

Stella's asleep on the couch, her own way of escaping. Helen, the nurse, diagnosed exhaustion. Lots of rest is what she needs but at least her ears are fine. But how's he going to tell her? The Torturer's just a baby. She doesn't know what death means — she'll keep looking for her mother.

'Dad, there's stuff I need to tell you.'

Jack looks gutted. 'What d'you mean?' he asks. 'Stuff about your mother?'

'This guy, Henry,' Von begins, 'he's been good to me and Stella. When Welfare was on my tail, he put us up at his place. We had a chat about the house, the one in Kaingaroa. Henry never believed that Charlene would be there. He's a pretty smart dude. He had his own theory.'

'Go on,' Jack urges.

Von tries to explain what lay behind Charlene's troubles. How Pete was dealing drugs until he was caught doing the dirty. 'He was selling speed to bikies but his partner didn't know it. Then he disappeared. His partner thought Mum was involved so he hit her for the money.'

Jack mulls the whole mess over. 'And your Mum never mentioned owning any property?'

'Not a word,' Von says. 'She was always working her butt off. But the last time Pete called her, Mum was working at Endorphin. He left this message about some trouble and said to mention Kaingaroa. Henry reckons it was Pete who bought the Kaingaroa place. He says the Chathams are miles from anywhere; you couldn't find a better hide-out. Maybe he put it in Mum's name because he's got a record.'

Jack shakes his head. He doesn't look convinced. 'Son, if that's the case, your mother must have known. She'd have to sign the transfer.' He explains that signatures have to be witnessed; a legal process must be followed. 'Remember how you told me Charlene's spent time on the Chathams. Pete may have mentioned Kaingaroa because he was hoping that she'd join him there.'

'Maybe,' Von says. 'But why would she deceive me?'

'I don't know,' Jack says. 'She may have had no choice. I'll call Detective Tapper in Wellington — he'll probably make some sense of this.'

'But if you tell the cops, they'll come and take Stella.'

'No they won't,' Jack says with authority. 'I'll make sure you stay together.'

Ahinata arrives to tell them dinner's ready. She takes Von's arm, leads him to the table.

'Von, I'm sure, right now, your head is filled with worries. But I know a way to help you clear your mind. There's a Moriori beach and it's right here at Henga. After we've eaten I'd be honoured to take you there — it often brings me comfort. If you listen carefully to the wind, you'll feel the ancestors come to you.' She turns to Jack, searching for his approval. 'Let me share this place with Von. Long Beach is very healing.'

Jack's not pleased with the suggestion. 'Are you sure that's a good idea? Son, you've just had bad news — don't you want to be with your family?'

'Dad, it's hard to explain but something's happened here on Rekohu. It's like the ancestors know — they've been trying to reach out to me. I'm scared shitless about Mum; nothing can make that go away. But karapuna feel like family and right now I need to be with them.'

Jack's eyes fill with tears when he folds Von in his arms. Their eyelids close as their noses come together. Von finally joins his father in a Moriori hongi.

Words are unnecessary; their eyes meet in understanding. There's nothing to explain. At last they share the same connection.

Staring across his desk, Tapper's nostrils start to flare. He has to stifle a sneeze as he reaches for a tissue. After loudly blowing his nose, he returns his focus to Henry.

'You've information, you say, about a woman called Charlene.'

'That's right,' Henry stalls, not sure how to answer. He's felt like shit since reading about Kristie. He remembers locking the shop, running up to Charlene's apartment, all the time hoping that somehow she would be there. She wasn't, of course, so he tried the Roos Roost. But the number's obviously faulty — he couldn't reach Von on the Chathams.

'Spit it out, then,' Tapper says. 'What sort of information?'

Henry picks his words carefully. 'The music store I manage, it's right below her apartment. Her son Von, he's a friend of mine — that's why I know she's missing. Charlene dances at Endorphin, that nightclub down on Vivian Street. The other night she started her shift. But she never came home again.'

The Endorphin case has been covered to death. Charlene and Endorphin have been splashed all over the paper.

'That's old news,' Tapper says. 'Anything else you'd like to tell me?'

Sensing an edge of impatience, Henry answers quickly. 'Charlene's boyfriend's a dealer — but I guess you know that too?'

Answering with his eyes, Tapper urges him to continue.

'I'm just scared Charlene's met the same fate as Kristie.'

'Don't tell me you know her too?'

'No, not really,' Henry says. 'I've just seen her at Endorphin. But the last time I was there, this dealer guy was bothering her. Von told me Kristie was a friend of his mum's. When Charlene went missing, he thought she might have stayed with her.'

'Interesting,' Tapper says. 'Son, I'm sure you know already, your friend's a missing person. We're very concerned — his life could be in danger.'

Overcome with nerves, Henry tugs on his dreads. 'He's okay,' he finally admits. 'I drove him to the airport.'

'Why?' Tapper shouts as his fist thumps onto the desk. 'Why, in God's name, didn't you tell us sooner?'

Henry tries to explain. He's never been a dobber. 'It's a trust thing,' he says. 'We're mates, it's like a promise. Von found a receipt made out to his mum. It says she's bought a house over on the Chathams.'

'You mean the Chatham Islands?'

'Yeah,' Henry says. 'Von's certain she's moved to this village called Kaingaroa. I thought I'd give him a few days, just in case he found her, but time's moving on and I haven't been able to reach him. Listen, I only came today because there's stuff you need to know.'

'Just tell me,' Tapper snaps, his patience wearing thin.

'Kristie looked shit-scared when I saw her with that dealer. I wanted to have a chat, see if she knew about Charlene but when I tried to find her later, she'd gone without a trace. I've seen this guy before hanging around Charlene — he's a seriously heavy customer.'

'Can you give us a detailed description? Help us draw up an identikit?'

'Of course,' Henry says. 'But first I need some reassurance.'

'Stop playing games. What sort of reassurance?'

'Just promise me, right, you'll go easy on Von. It'll tear the guy apart if you take his little sister.'

Shivers course down his spine as they enter the grove. It's like stepping through a gateway to an ancient dimension. Moments ago, they were bathed in brilliant light; the moon mirrored on the surface of Lake Marakapia. But in the forest behind the lodge, black shadows enfold them. They're following a path that winds between the trees. Ahinata shows the way. Von's glad she brought the torches.

As they weave between the kopis, the silvery trees seem wraith-like; their gentle, shivery motions appearing almost human. A haunting cry echoes through the night. He hears the snap of breaking twigs — something's charging through the undergrowth.

Ahinata turns and smiles. 'Just a weka,' she assures him. Soon a small flightless bird dashes across their pathway. Deeper in the grove they reach a cluster of rock formations. Moss-covered bones lie scattered in the leaf litter; an eerie stillness fills the place — it makes Von feel uneasy. Did his ancestors die here? Is this the site of another massacre?

'Are they human?' he asks. Ahinata shakes her head. 'Albatross,' she says. 'Karapuna often ate them. The large bones are bovine — farmers used to graze their cattle here.'

They tramp through the dunes that lead down to the ocean. Ahinata shines her torch on a scattered pile of sea shells.

'A midden,' she explains. 'They're all through these dunes.'

As they move towards the beach, the wind grabs Von's attention. He gulps the salty air; hears the crash of waves. The ocean looks black and endless — like the void that devours him when he thinks about his mother.

Grit shifts beneath his feet as they trudge the Henga foreshore. Their path is splashed with silver. Daggers of moonlight stab through a drifting cloud bank. A smooth black rock is lying in the shallows. Ahinata gets excited as she makes her way towards it.

'A pilot whale,' she cries. 'I'll need to contact Conservation. But first I'll ring the elders; our people will come and help it.'

Von rolls up his jeans and wades towards the creature. It looks distressed; water spurts from its blowhole. Cupping his hands, he fills them with seawater. Then he gently showers the whale, hoping the water soothes it. As their eyes connect, the moment is almost dream-like. But soon a new wave of dread threatens to engulf him. Whales signify death — is this some kind of omen? What if the stranding happened here because Charlene's been murdered?

'It's a sign,' he says, turning to Ahinata. She takes his hands, tries to reassure him. 'No,' she insists, 'your mother isn't Moriori. If anyone sent this whale, it was probably old Sam. His funeral's being held in Waitangi tomorrow. It's time I left,' she adds quietly. 'You need some time alone now. When you're ready to return just follow the path I showed you. Stay close to the whale, pay attention to the wind. Karapuna are here but only if you listen.'

Ahinata leaves and he turns to face the ocean. Gusts whip along the beach, ferocious and unrelenting. The wind's blowing him away; it's offended by his presence. As he squats in the shallows next to the stranded whale, Von's thoughts are with Charlene. A thousand fears still haunt him. In the past, when things weren't right, he would get some kind of warning. Like that awful day when Stella got so frightened. Something told him she was scared; he just knew he had to help her. Since his mother disappeared he's been a total wreck and he'd be mad not to think that she's in a heap of trouble. But not once has he experienced one of those weird *knowing* signs. Von's sure if she was dead that somehow he would feel it.

The moon dips behind the clouds and suddenly he's blanketed in darkness. Hairs rise sharply on the back of his neck; the wind is alive — he's shivering all over. They are here; he can feel them — the spirits of his ancestors. Then, softly, the moon starts to brush the sand with silver. He sees her face in every shell, her mane of messy curls in each glistening strand of seaweed. Her aura surfs into shore on the crest of every wave. Charlene's presence is everywhere; his mother is all around him. *Karapuna chant — he starts listening to his instincts.* Picking up a piece of driftwood, he carves letters in the sand. Big, bold, beautiful letters — letters she would love, letters spiralling like music. Then the moon beams down and those letters shine like stars. And, at last, he understands what they're trying to show him. Her name lights up the beach, it's glowing with her life-force.

He closes his eyes, feels his spirit spiral upwards. As he soars through the sky, Von is the mighty albatross. The whispering lips of gods caress his feathery wing tips; they are passing on their wisdom, sharing all their secrets. The ancestors are with him, guiding him on his journey. Below, on the beach, he can see his earthly body. They have set his spirit free. There's something they must show him.

A solitary seagull circles above a cruiser. It swoops then soars in a wave of lost confusion. Karapuna lead the way, now they dive towards the boat. Von feels his mother's energy — he's certain that she's down there.

His eyes are wide open. He's standing on the beach. The whale has gone and a peaceful calm surrounds him.

Charlene Taiaroa is alive. This is not the name of a dead woman.

Drifting now — her essence takes flight. The pain has gone; the blindness and the hunger. She sees her own damaged body, still bound and gagged in the battered boat below her. An angel's feather brushes her — it whispers of new life. She feels the healing warmth of love as it floods through her soul. Now Von's voice is all around her, she hears his heartbeat singing. Then she remembers her little girl, feels her tender baby kisses. Charlene glides above her body and knows the choice is hers. Will she return to her life and fight? Or will she leave them behind and follow the light force?

'It was mind-blowing, Dad, like her soul reached out and touched me. There's no way she can be dead. Believe me, I know it.'

Last night, before the beach, Von was visibly in pain; so shocked by the news that he couldn't eat a morsel. Now Jack's hearing a whole new person as his son tucks into a flounder.

After each mouthful, Von tries to explain what happened. 'There's more,' he says. 'I don't know if you'll believe me.' His eyes look haunted as he relives the experience. 'Karapuna came; my spirit left my body. When we soared above the clouds, in my mind, I was an albatross.'

Von was out the whole night on that isolated beach, with nothing but the wind and the moon for company. Jack's more than aware of the stress the boy's been under. What's happening to his son? Is he suffering from delusions? An albatross, he thinks, as he tries to make sense of things. They're spiritually significant in Moriori culture. Von would know that, for sure. Perhaps he's been hallucinating.

'An albatross?' he says. 'They're very special to our people. But how can you be so sure that your mother is alive?'

Von puts down his fork. He looks a bit embarrassed. 'I know this all sounds weird; there's no easy way to explain it. When I flew with karapuna, they took me to a boat. I'm certain that's where Mum is — I could really feel her energy.'

Before Jack can respond, the phone rings behind the bar. Jean must have heard it in the kitchen — she rushes through to get it.

Jack looks at Von as they listen in discreetly. Jean's brow is creased with worry — she's not happy with what she's hearing. 'That's disturbing,' she says, 'but you need to stay put. It's easier for me to tell them.'

After clearing her throat, Jean comes over to the table. 'That was Ahinata. A police squad's just flown in from Wellington. They're on Waitangi beach — a body's washed ashore there.'

His heart's being ripped apart; he can't handle any more of this. Were the ancestors too late when they took him on that journey? Was his mum already gone when her spirit somehow touched him? Stan tears up the dirt as they race towards Waitangi. Stella's back at the lodge with Helen and Jean. They said a crime scene on the beach was no place for a toddler. Jack sits next to Von, trying to be optimistic.

'Son, don't lose heart now; trust what karapuna showed you.'

He's still haunted by that seagull — sees it circling above the boat. In that one surreal moment, he knew Charlene was down there. That's probably why he's scared. It's been hours since his experience. Did the angry ocean take her? Has she finally washed ashore here?

He turns to his dad; there's no better time to show him. 'Mum gave me this shark's tooth; she found it on the Chathams. She told me herself — she really loved Rekohu.'

Jack's expression is glum as he plays with the tooth. He loved her once. Von wonders what he's feeling. 'Dad, this morning, at breakfast, when I told you about the beach, I could see it in your face — you didn't really believe me. But now you're being so positive. Are you trying to protect me?'

Jack looks evasive. He takes a while to answer. 'Maybe,' he says. 'But I've been thinking instead of feeling. You've been through so much — I thought you were hallucinating. But then I remembered how karapuna found me. My dad was ill in Wellington when I first heard them calling. Some things you can't explain. You've got to trust in what you're feeling.'

Von's emotions are confused, he's unsure of what he's feeling. He was a mess when he decided to come and meet his mum. Just the thought of seeing her made him feel so nervous. He didn't know who she was or even if he'd like her, and after they met she kept pushing him to the limit. They took a while to gel but then this fragile link of love gradually formed between them. Charlene's part of who he is — in a way, that's what he's fighting for. And it was tough, at first, being stuck with little Stella. But now they've shared an incredible journey, he can't imagine life without her.

'Stella's sweet,' Jack says, as if he's read Von's mind. 'And she's strong,' he adds, 'the way she's coped with all this trouble.'

But how strong, Von wonders. Her dad's a wanted criminal and her mum's in heaps of trouble. Jack says to trust karapuna, believe Charlene's alive. But that's no guarantee he's ever going to find her.

Stan slowly drives the bus onto the beach. A large group of people have gathered on the foreshore. Von spots a bunch of men in suits — probably the Wellington detectives. A little further up the coast is a taped-off area. His head starts to swim and he searches for a lolly. For one scary moment he thinks he's having a hypo. Now a beefy guy in a suit comes across to join them.

'Jack Taiaroa,' the man says, looking surprised. 'I wasn't expecting to see you here.'

'Likewise,' Jack answers. He's obviously embarrassed. 'I'm sorry,' he adds. 'I've been meaning to call you. Son,' he turns to Von. 'This is Detective Tapper.'

Von shakes Tapper's hand. The detective's expression isn't happy.

'You've certainly given us the run-around. Where've you hidden your little sister?'

'She's fine,' Jack cuts in before Von can answer. 'Stella's safe with friends — he's been taking good care of her.'

Tapper points his chunky finger at the looming taped-off area. 'Son, this is going to be hard; I wish we could avoid it. But we need identification and you may be able to help us.'

What's he trying to tell him? Have they found his mother's body? Emerging from the crowd, Ahinata takes Von's arm. Tapper clears his throat before speaking again.

'The body was found first thing this morning. The deceased is male, most probably Caucasian.'

The relief is indescribable; it's flooding all Von's senses. But Tapper hasn't finished. 'We're almost certain it's Pete Mullins, your mother's partner.'

Relief is replaced by a gnawing sense of sadness. Von only spoke to Pete twice, but he was Stella's father.

'We've got access to photos and we're checking dental records. But I was wondering if you could identify him.'

'I'm sorry,' Von explains, 'but we never actually met. Mum showed me a few snapshots; I suppose I could take a look at him.'

'That's not necessary,' Tapper says. 'If you don't know the

man, there's no need to go through that ordeal.'

Von's thoughts are with Stella. Pete Mullins is her father. 'He's my little sister's dad. Would it be okay if I said goodbye for her?'

When the detective nods, they start walking towards the body. As Tapper lifts the sheet of plastic, Von takes in the bloated features. His eyes drift downwards and his stomach does a lurch. There's a gull in full flight etched into one forearm. It's beautiful work — he's looking at the Seagull. His mind slides back to the flight with karapuna, to the lonely, circling seagull crying above the boat. Did Pete's spirit reach Charlene too? Was he trying to connect with her?

His legs give out; he collapses on the sand.

'What's up?' A voice asks. It sounds far away and foggy.

'We need a doctor,' Jack yells. 'I think he's having a hypo.'

'I'm fine,' Von says, recovering. He's embarrassed by all the fussing. 'Just seeing someone so lifeless — my head went kinda fuzzy.'

'Are you sure?' Tapper says. 'There's help here if you need it.'

Von shakes his head. Ahinata offers him some water. After taking a couple of swigs, he feels a bit more normal. 'It's probably Pete,' he says to Tapper. 'Mum mentioned the tattoo — his nickname was the Seagull.'

Jack and the cop walk a distance away together. Ahinata stays with Von. They take in the scene together.

'Poor Stella,' she says quietly. 'She's too young to lose her father.'

Or her mum, Von thinks. Now he really needs to find her.

Stella probably lost Pete the day he set up that lab. Still, it was nothing like this. Death is so final.

'Von, that house in Kaingaroa — I finally heard from the lawyer. All the negotiations were done by Pete Mullins. But the title deed says it belongs to your mother.'

Thoughts of betrayal torment him once again. But his heart says something different — Charlene wouldn't have deceived him. Henry was probably right and Pete bought it as a getaway. But the bikie's still a mystery — Von's not sure what to make of that.

'It's strange,' he says to Ahinata. 'I'm not convinced she knew anything about it. Maybe Pete tricked my mum into signing for the property.'

Tapper and Jack tramp through the sand towards them. The detective sits down and looks at Von gravely. 'There've been a few developments regarding your mother.'

'Have you found her?' Von asks. He knows he's being hopeful.

'No, I'm sorry,' Tapper says. 'But we've received new information. We now have a definite suspect for the murder of Kristie Nichol — Pete Mullins, the deceased, was very closely linked to him. Furthermore, it would appear the suspect knows your mother.'

This sounds like Detective Henry. He must have been to see him. Tapper's still talking but Von no longer hears him. Charlene's essence was on that boat; they connected on some level.

He knows she's still alive — he's got to trust karapuna.

'There's more.' Tapper says. Von tries to pay attention.

'The suspect found Mullins hiding up the coast. He'd been

living in a property that belongs to your mother. Another fellow was staying in the house — he tipped us off just a few hours ago. It would appear the suspect kidnapped your mother to put pressure on Pete Mullins.'

It all makes sense, especially about the bikie. Ahinata was suspicious; she never believed his story. The guy was covering for Pete — Charlene obviously never made it there. Von's thoughts turn to Kristie. He's still confused about her role in this.

'Was Kristie helping Mum? Is that why she was murdered?'

'We're not certain,' Tapper shrugs, 'but they were close friends. It's likely they'd share secrets. The suspect is known at Endorphin — he'd have seen the women together. If your mother refused to cooperate after he took her hostage, he may have turned to Kristie to get his information. I'm sorry,' the detective says. 'It's not a good scenario. We're trying to find out where the suspect hid your mother. But now that Mullins has been found dead, we don't hold out a lot of hope for her.'

Henry's still half-asleep as he waits for the morning forecast. Heavy rain's been drenching Wellington for at least a couple of days. His spirit craves a bit of sun; a day twenty degrees or over. After dobbing Von in to Tapper, his mood's been like the weather. There wasn't any choice but he still feels like a traitor. He can't stop thinking about those kids, wondering how they're going. He just prays Von's found his mum and Welfare can stop chasing them.

Good morning, the newsreader says as the radio alarm kicks in. *We've got all the hottest stories on 89FM.* Henry's still half-asleep; he often dozes through the news. But then Charlene's name jolts him out of his inertia … *a boat was found drifting off Palliser Bay. The woman on board had been seriously assaulted. Reports from Wellington Hospital say her condition is critical. Police have yet to confirm if the woman is Charlene Taiaroa, the missing dancer in the Endorphin dance club case.*

Henry throws back his quilt; quickly pulls on his jeans. Minutes later he's heading for the hospital.

'Please,' she tries to say. 'Don't want to do that any more …'

She takes a clumsy swipe — someone's trying to inject her. But the pounding in her brain nearly makes her pass out again. Her vision is blurry, the whole room is swimming. A man fades in and out of her ever changing focus.

'Just relax,' she hears him say. 'It's going to take the edge off things.'

She feels the drug kick in as she desperately clings to consciousness, and realises, now, that she must be in a hospital. In the corner of her vision there's an intravenous drip. She starts to dry retch, overcome with pain and nausea.

The throbbing in her head gradually subsides — she floats away on an iridescent ocean. Lights above her bed shine down on her like stars. She blinks away some fog and they flicker out of sight again. The shadow of someone tall is hovering by her side. Charlene grips his hand, convinced her son is standing there.

'I'm so sorry, Von. I never meant to hurt you.'

Gently squeezing back, Henry tries to reassure her. Then he feels her grip go as she drifts back to her ocean.

A new day is dawning on the ancient land of Rekohu. Von walks the shore of Long Beach sharing Henga with his father.

'So this is where it happened?'

'Right here,' Von says as he wades into the shallows. 'They came on the wind — this is where I heard their voices.'

A warm breeze blows today. The atmosphere is different. But he knows they're still around; he can hear their gentle whispers. In his heart he's still an albatross gliding lofty thermals, searching for his mother with the help of karapuna. Rob had left her on the boat when he took off for the Chathams. She must have clung to life for days, a lonely drifter on the ocean.

'It's a mystery,' Jack says, 'the way this whole thing turned out. They knew she was alive and you had the strength to trust them.'

Charlene's voice was barely there when Von spoke to her at the hospital. But Henry took the phone and acted as a go-between — she knew Pete was on the Chathams but nothing about her home there. Her condition is improving, though she's got a way to go, but she'll never be safe as long as Rob's still out there. Tapper says they're getting close; won't be long before they nab him. But Von knows she won't relax until he's locked up in the slammer.

Charlene's been to hell and back; she needs her kids around her. He's aching to see Juice, she's always on his mind, but he can't leave little Stella while their mother's still in hospital.

'So,' Jack says, quietly. 'Where do we go from here?'

'We've already had this conversation. You know I'm going to stay in Wellington.'

Jack's face says it all. Von's sure he's going to lose it. 'Son, you have to face reality. You're sixteen years old — you won't get custody of your sister.'

Von hasn't slept for days and he's not in the mood to argue. 'We should head back; the plane leaves in a couple of hours. I need to pack for Stella — can we talk about it later?'

'Please,' Jack says, aware he's getting the brush-off. 'Your sister needs an adult who can take proper care of her.'

'But that's exactly what I've done for the last few weeks. The whole time I've been in Wellington, I've taken care of Stella.'

'I know,' Jack says. 'I'm not trying to be negative. And believe me, son, I'm really very proud of you. But your mum has serious injuries. Even when she's ready to leave the hospital, it could be weeks before she's strong enough to look after Stella.'

'Are you talking about foster care?'

'Of course not,' Jack sighs, as he picks up a pebble. He folds it in his palm then hurls it at the ocean. 'Son, I'm not sure how to say this. I've been doing a lot of soul searching. Maybe it's being here at Henga; your experience with karapuna. But there's things we can't control. I don't know if we're really meant to.'

He's not sure what Jack means — why can't he spell it out for him?

'When your mum went off the rails, I didn't give her many choices. You'd been hurt, I was angry — we were on a downward spiral. When she flew off to the clinic, she didn't know that I still loved her.'

Von remembers Charlene's words when she told him why she left — how Jack didn't want her back unless she sorted out her habit. It might have taken years but she finally quit amphetamines. She was totally clean when he first arrived in Wellington.

'She'd beaten it, Dad. She only fell off the wagon when the strife with Pete turned heavy.'

'Yes, I've made a few mistakes. Don't want to make another one.'

Von searches his father's eyes, looking for an answer.

'Son, your sister's lost her father — she really needs stability. I'm applying for special leave; we could find a place to stay in Wellington. When your mother's fit and well again, we can reassess the situation.'

Von's heart fills up — he didn't know Jack had it in him. Taking time off work to help with little Stella. 'Are you sure you're really up for this?'

'It wouldn't be right to split you up now. You're a family,' Jack says. 'And your baby sister loves you.'

He feels the presence of the ancestors as he walks back through the kopis. Kamapuna were with him every step of his journey. They taught him how to trust — now they're always going to be with him. If Charlene moves to Rekohu, he'd like to show her Henga. Ahinata was right — there's comfort in the air here. Over the last few weeks they've all faced their own invasions. But the light, the birdsong; there's real magic in this grove.

Von lets his eyes close and, once again, he is the albatross.

His mighty wings spread out.

Let this feeling last forever.

ACKNOWLEDGEMENTS

Special thanks to my wonderful husband, Dave Kell, who first told me about the Moriori and for being a wise and valued reader, and to the Hokotehi Moriori Trust for endorsing my work in this novel. Enormous gratitude goes to Maui Solomon, Denise Davis, Wilf Davis and Shirley King for generously sharing their Moriori knowledge and experiences. I'm also deeply indebted to the late Michael King for the historical and cultural information found in his book *Moriori: A People Rediscovered* (Revised Edition), Penguin Books. Thanks to Rhys Richards for his work on the Moriori language, Paul Dessauer for information on amphetamines and Derek Le Dayn for his detailed descriptions of the cityscape of Wellington.

A huge thank you to Angelina Kell for reconnecting me with my inner two year old, to Sarah Watson for sharing her rich knowledge of dance club culture, Megan Watson for her invaluable feedback and many hours of babysitting, and Nathan Watson for his ongoing support and encouragement.

Thank you to ArtsWA for funding the project and providing me with an Artflight to Rekohu, and also my deep appreciation goes to Clive Newman and Ray Coffey for believing in this story.

Finally, thanks to all the people who gave me love and encouragement during the writing of *mama's trippin*.

More information on the Moriori can be found on the Te Ara Encyclopedia of New Zealand website at:

> www.teara.govt.nz/NewZealanders/
> MaoriNewZealanders/Moriori/en

Also by Katy Watson-Kell

JUICE

Jenna Stewart — Juice — and her friends, are young athletes with dreams of success at the highest level. Juice has her sights set on gold in the Olympic one hundred metres, but rivalry with her oldest friend Sam, the demands of school, her mother's embarrassing secret, and the imminent departure of her accordion-playing gran threaten to get in the way.

And then there's Von — at first they're just training partners but something happens, and suddenly Juice can't get him out of her mind.

Praise for *Juice*

Something for every reader — *Magpies*
An honest and insightful look at teenagers — *West Australian*
The author writes from the heart — *ETA Notes*

Juice received the Avis Page Award for the most popular Australian novel in the Older Readers category in the West Australian Young Readers Book Awards in 2002.